The Little Cottage Shop and Two Little Urchins

David A Prosser

Pen Press

© David A Prosser 2012

All rights reserved

No part of this publication may be reproduced, stored in a retrieval system, or transmitted in any form or by any means, without the prior permission in writing of the publisher, nor be otherwise circulated in any form of binding or cover other than that in which it is published and without a similar condition including this condition being imposed on the subsequent purchaser.

First published in Great Britain by Pen Press

All paper used in the printing of this book has been made from wood grown in managed, sustainable forests.

ISBN: 978-1-78003-293-1

Printed and bound in the UK
Pen Press is an imprint of
Indepenpress Publishing Limited
25 Eastern Place
Brighton
BN2 1GJ

A catalogue record of this book is available from
the British Library

Cover design by Jacqueline Abromeit

Illustrations Graham Wilson

I dedicate this book to my four grandchildren
Holly, Scott, Joanne and Lauren
and my two great grandchildren
Taylor and Sian

My grateful thanks to the artist
Graham Wilson
for all the artwork in this book

My grateful thanks
to my publisher
Grace Rafael
for her dedication and patience
in producing books for
everyone to enjoy.

Contents

The Little Cottage Shop

Christmas Day

In the 1940s, as a little boy age 5 David always wanted a train set and farm yard animals so he could make it look like a real countryside setting. Nearly every Christmas all of fhis friends got something to do with trains; all David could do was hope that one Christmas his dream would come true.

Johnny, one of David's friends, got a beautiful German train set made by Bing; his nanny and granddad bought him three coaches that were blood and custard in colour, yellow and top and red on the bottom. Trevor, David's other friend, had a beautiful Princess Elizabeth made by Hornby; it was in a beautiful long red box with a blue velvet interior; it was second hand but it was still in mint condition. This was his granddad's and he had bought it himself in 1937 for five pounds and five shillings and then he gave it to Trevor, his only grandson, with lots of track and points and two wonderful Pullman coaches all still in their original boxes. Trevor's granddad had never played with this train set, he had set it up in the loft for Trevor and Trevor never knew he was doing it because he wasn't allowed up there.

After Christmas dinner David, Trevor and Johnny met up on the street corner, as children do, and asked each other what Father Christmas had bought them. Of course, they didn't really believe in Father Christmas but it was just a bit of a joke. Johnny had bought out his boxed set of trains.

"Cor," said David. "That's great. I wish I had one like that."

"What did you have, Dave?" asked Trevor.

"Nothing this year, my mom hadn't any spare money to buy presents, she told us that with six children to feed it's better to eat than to play with toys."

"Your parents are mean, Dave," Johnny replied.

"No, they ain't," David answered. "I had a bar of chocolate all to myself."

Johnny laughed. "A bar? A bar of chocolate? I had a big box of chocolates off my aunty *and* a present. A bar," he giggled.

"Take no notice, Dave. You are horrible," said Trevor to Johnny. "You never laughed at him when he earned that two and sixpence and he shared it with us."

"What's that got to do with anything?" Johnny asked, pulling a face.

"Are we going to see the train running, Johnny?" David asked.

"No way, I'm not letting you touch my train set, I don't want it scratched."

"I won't touch it, Johnny. I just want to see it running."

"No, I'm going home now to play with it," and with a smirk he added, "and to eat some of my chocolates that my aunty bought for me."

David was feeling very hurt and was fighting to hold back the tears.

"We don't want to play with your rotten train," Trevor shouted. David was thinking I do, Oh I wish I had a train set.

"David, you won't believe it but my granddad made a layout for the train set he gave me for Christmas. It's in the loft; lots of track and points. You want to see the scenery, Dave? It's brilliant."

David's eyes went wide with excitement.

"Do you think your mom and dad would let me see your trains, Trev?"

"Come on, I'll ask them."

"Oh thanks, Trev. I don't know why Johnny was so horrible, do you?"

"He's always like that, he likes showing off. Remember when he had that new bike for his birthday? He was telling everyone how rich his parents were, remember?"

"Oh yes, he was horrible that day weren't he, Trev?"

"He was, Dave."

So off they went to Trevor's house.

As they got to the back door Trevor said, "Wait here, I'll ask if it's all right for you to come in."

I bet they'll say no, David was thinking to himself. David knew Trevor's mom and dad didn't like him very much; he had heard them saying one day how dirty and scruffy he was so he really thought they would say no.

Trevor came out and invited him in the house. David was shocked but excited at the thought of seeing Trevor's layout.

"Merry Christmas," David said to Trevor's family as he walked into their lounge.

A roaring fire, a Christmas tree, food on the table, cakes, jelly, blancmange, apples and oranges; it all looked so posh and plentiful to David, he had never seen so much food in one house before.

"Merry Christmas, David," Trevor's granddad greeted him as he walked in.

Trevor's mom and dad just looked at him with a sort of disapproving look.

Granddad said, "It is David isn't it?"

"Yes," replied David in a timid voice.

"I thought it was but I wasn't sure. What did Father Christmas bring you for Christmas, David?" asked Granddad.

"Nothing, sir, my mom had no money for presents, only for food. It's better I eat than play with toys, my mom said," David answered.

Trevor's granddad felt really bad for asking. "What about your nanny and granddad, did they not buy you anything?"

"They were killed in the war; their house was bombed," as he told him, a tear ran down David's face.

Trevor's granddad felt full of guilt now. "I'm sorry, son. Here's two shillings for you as a Christmas box."

"Oh thank you, sir," David said. A very big smile came across his face as he wiped the tears away from his cheeks. This is a real Christmas now!

Trevor's granddad gave David a handful of sweets and said, "When you are ready to go home, I'll give you some cake."

"Thank you so much, sir," David said.

"Now you go and play with Trevor's new train set."

"Cor, thank you."

Well, David flew up the stairs; he just couldn't wait to see the trains.

"Ooh-er, Trev, it's brilliant."

"It is," Trevor replied.

"I love it. What's the loco called?"

"It's called a Lizzie, my granddad said."

"Lizzie?"

"Yes, that's short for Elizabeth."

"Oh, I didn't know that."

"Nor me until Granddad said," Trevor replied.

"Wish I had a train set. If I run lots of errands and save the money I could buy one."

"Don't be daft, Dave, it would take for ever. Look how it snakes going through the points, Dave."

David was very jealous.

"Do you like these dinky cars, a break down lorry, a lorry with a flat back and a box with five different cars in the set? I'm going to put them around the layout."

"Oh yes," said David. "That would look good."

Two hours had passed when Trevor's mom called him down for his tea.

As they walked to the front door, Trevor's granddad said, "David, there are some sweets and fruit in the bag for you and a nice piece of cake."

"Thank you very much and thank you for letting me see the trains."

"You are welcome," he shouted from the lounge as David was closing the front door.

David ran home and told his brothers and sisters all about Trevor's train layout and he explained in detail what the scenery looked like.

"I've got some sweets and fruit, Mom you can share them around. You have some as well, Mom."

"You are kind," she replied.

"Well, you've told us we must look after each other and always be kind and well mannered, haven't you, Mom?"

"That's right, David," his mother said.

They were all very excited when they had two sweets each and a segment of orange.

"Where's Dad, Mom?" David asked.

"You might know; in bed sleeping it off." By "off" she meant he was drunk. That's why they were poor; all the money went on beer. Their dad only cared about himself.

The Garden Job

A few days later as he was walking down the road, David passed two ladies who were stood talking.

As he passed, he heard one of the ladies say, "It's a real shame that lad never had any toys for Christmas."

How would they know that? thought David.

The next day, a lady at the top of David's road called him.

"David, can I see you for a minute?"

When he got to her she asked him if he would do some gardening for her.

"I'll pay you one shilling and sixpence."

Christmas had finally come for David.

"Yes, missus, I will," he replied excitedly. "What would you like me to do?"

"Cut the grass and edge it with the shears, and trim the hedge."

She came back with the gardening tools and laid them on the grass. Then she turned to David and said, "Did you have a nice Christmas?"

"Oh yes," replied David. "My friend Trevor had a great big layout in the roof, his granddad did it for him. He had cars and everything and we played trains for ages and ages."

"That was nice for you. And what did you have for Christmas?"

"Shall I start to mow the grass, missus?"

"Don't you want to tell me what you had?"

With his head bent and in a very low voice he answered, "Nothing."

"Speak up. I can't hear what you are saying."

"I didn't have anything. My mom said she didn't have any money to waste on presents, it's better to eat than play with toys."

"Oh you poor boy. Look, my son is in the army now, he's too big to play with toys, and I've still got his toys from when he was a little boy. I'll sort you some out whilst you are doing the garden."

"Oh, thank you."

Toys! I'm going to get toys! All his nerves trembled with excitement.

David worked very hard and after he had cleaned up and put the tools away, the lady said, "Did you clean the tools before you put them away?"

"Yes, missus, I wiped them with an old rag like you told me to."

"Good lad. Here are some toys for you. I've tied the box up so nothing will drop out."

David's heart was racing he was so excited. When he saw how big the box was he was even more excited and when he tried to pick it up he found he couldn't lift it.

"Oh dear," said the lady. "It's too heavy for you to lift. I'll take some out."

Not likely, David thought, so with every ounce of strength he could muster, by holding the strings on the box and with a huge deep breath, he lifted the box. Unable to speak, he staggered down the path, got just outside onto the pavement behind the hedge where the lady couldn't see him and dropped the box. His lungs where at full stretch and he could hardly breathe. I'll drag it, he thought, and so he did, a little at a time.

"It's flipping heavy," he said to himself. "I wonder what's in it." He went to open it, but then thought, I'd better not, I'll get it home first.

It took him 20 minutes to get it halfway to his house. Right, I'll really try harder now. Little did he know the box was almost ready to fall apart because he had been dragging it and just as he started to drag it again, he felt a pain in his back; a boy had poked him in the back with a stick.

"Hey, what you got there, where did you pinch that from?"

“I never pinched it. I worked for it,” replied David.

The other boy who was with him started to push David.

“Leave me alone, I haven’t done anything to you.”

“You’re a liar.” As he was speaking he kept pushing him while the other boy was poking him with a stick.

”We’re having this box and there’s nothing you can do about it.” As he was saying this, he kept slapping David around the face. With his last ounce of energy, David, out of shear fear and the worry of losing the box, clenched his fist and punch the boy on the nose. His nose split wide open, the bones shattered and blood flew everywhere. The boy with the stick looked in horror, feeling sick he staggered backwards.

“I’m—I’m going to tell his mom.” So off he ran. The other boy was holding his nose and screaming.

David felt frightened and didn’t know what to do, with all the screaming going on the neighbours come running out of their houses to see what was going on. It was a shock to everyone to see this boy covered in blood and screaming. The boy’s mother arrived and in sheer panic she grabbed hold of David and shook him violently and started to slap him so hard he fainted.

A neighbour caught hold of her arm.

“Stop it! Stop it! You’ll kill him! It’s not his fault, it’s your son’s fault and his mate. They started tormenting David for no good reason. David didn’t even say a word to them.”

“Look at him his nose is split wide open. Get an ambulance! GET AN AMBULANCE! Please, my son is dying!” she was screaming. She was now in a rage and grabbed David again, screaming at him. She punched him in the face.

“You dirty, horrible boy.”

Two men who had joined in to see what was going on got hold of the lady and dragged her off David, who by this time was covered in blood and his nose was bleeding.

David’s mom came running over to him crying and wiping blood from his face and saying, “My baby, my baby.”

The police and the ambulance pulled up at the same time, they saw to the other boy first and put him in the ambulance and then looked at David. He only had a nose bleed and they brought him round with smelling salts.

The other boy's mother still very angry and was shouting as she was getting into the ambulance, "I'm going to have him put away. I'll go and see a solicitor in the morning."

The police officer made her get into the ambulance and he shut the door.

"How do you feel now, son?"

"I'm OK, sir," David replied.

"Can you tell me what happened?"

"Yes, sir. I was dragging this box that this lady gave to me," he said, pointing to the lady whose garden he had done.

"Is that right, missus?" asked the police officer.

"Yes. He is such a well-mannered boy, I can't imagine what's gone on. He only left me about an hour ago, maybe a littlie less."

The neighbour who lived next door but one from David's house said, "I saw it all. I was cleaning my bedroom windows."

David, pointing, added, "That boy was hitting me with a stick."

"I never! I never! He's lying."

"You're the one that's lying, young man. When I was cleaning the windows," the lady said, pointing across the road to her house, "that boy came up behind David and hit him in the back with a stick. Then he threw it over the hedge as he ran away. The other boy started to push David and kept slapping him and that boy kept hitting him with the stick. I didn't know what they were saying but then suddenly David, after being slapped and hit with a stick, punched the boy in the nose."

"What?" said the policeman. "One punch that's all?"

"Yes, officer," the lady said. "I heard the boy scream and then there was blood everywhere."

When the officer turned to the boy to question him, he broke down and cried his eyes out.

"OK, son, tell me the truth now."

"It's true, we picked on him. I was hitting him with my stick and I threw it over that hedge," he was pointing as he said it, "as I was running to get my friend's mom. It's our fault, I'm sorry, I'm sorry," he sobbed.

"Well, missus, do you wish to press charges?" the officer asked David's mother.

"No," David's mom said. "David has been through enough."

The boy who had hit David with a stick was made to look David in the eye and apologise.

David's mom explained to the officer, "I'd like them to be taken to the police station and be disciplined."

"We will," replied the officer.

"Good, I don't want any more said about it now."

The officer picked up the box and carried it to the house; after all that David had been through he still couldn't wait to open the box.

He said to his mom, "I'm sorry, Mom, I didn't mean to hurt that boy."

"He deserved it," she answered.

"I'm never going to hit anyone again."

David's brother said, "You are strong you know. I bet you would be a good boxer. I never knew you could punch like that."

"No, I don't want to be a boxer, I don't like hurting people. I just want to see what that lady has given to me."

With hands trembling from excitement, David started to undo the string. It was tied so tightly that it took him nearly 15 minutes to get the knot undone. David thought that the string was good so decided to keep it and not cut it, and he put it under his bed. As he lifted the flaps of the box it was like rays of sunshine escaping, as there, sitting on top of a pile of toys was a blue box with the words "British" and "Guaranteed". This was a Hornby train set. It said "Mo Train Set" on the end of the box. His hands were still trembling as he took off the lid, and there in all its glory, in mint condition, was a green loco, two coaches and silver track. The black sleepers made the silver rails shine out. David was so happy; a little tear ran down his cheek. He had lost control by this time; all the excitement became too much for him.

Just as David was hugging his loco to his chest, in walked Mom, "Oh my word, that is a beautiful train set."

She hugged David and asked him if he was OK.

"That lady is very kind, Mom, isn't she?"

"She most certainly is," replied Mom. "You must take care of them and always put them away tidy so as not to scratch them and remember to go and thank the lady for her kindness."

"Oh, I will, Mom, and I'll keep these toys for ever."

All the toys in that box were more toys than that house had ever seen.

David very carefully replaced the lid back onto the base of his new train set.

"I'll play with this train as soon as I see what else is in this box."

As he moved a piece of cardboard that had been placed there for the protection of all the toys, a long red box with horses printed on it was under the piece of card. When David took off the lid there were six black horses with guards sitting on them, all in perfect condition. Under that box were three boxes with marching soldiers, the same ones as the ones on the horses. David's heart was beating very fast; his little body couldn't take it all in. As he looked further into the box, he saw 14 Dinky cars and lorries. Holding one of the Dinkys, he sat on the floor breathing very hard.

The excitement was overwhelming him and gripping the Dinky car very tightly, he leaned against the wall, closed his eyes and fell asleep for nearly two hours and woke up with pins and needles in his legs and a numb bottom. He started to look into the box again and there, on the bottom, was a big triang crane with a bucket for lifting up soil and sand or whatever a boy wanted to lift up. David turned the different handles, one to raise the arm with the bucket on the end and one to lower it; there was even one to rotate the whole body round. It was red and green and again in mint condition.

David's mom told him to go and thank the lady for being so kind to him.

"I'll go tomorrow, Mom, and I'll do her garden for nothing."

Running Errands

The next morning David went to thank the lady. She was so pleased he had taken the trouble to go and thank her that she gave him a piece of cake.

"I'm glad you are all right. Those bullies deserved what you did. I'll sort you some more toys out over the weekend; I'll ask my husband to take them out of the loft," she told him.

"Oh, thank you, missus. Do you want anything from the shops?" David asked her.

"Yes please, you could get me some potatoes and six eggs. Four pounds of potatoes I think will be enough. Get them from Browns the Greengrocers."

"OK," said David. He ran all the way and when he got back and handed the lady the change, she said, "There you are, three pence for fetching my groceries."

"No, it's OK, missus. I'll do your garden for nothing as well," David told her.

"You are a kind lad. I am very grateful to you," she told him.

David now ran all the way down the hill to call for his friend Trevor and to tell him about his good fortune.

Trevor said, "I heard about the trouble you had. Did you really smash that boy's nose?"

"Yes. I didn't mean to, I never knew I was that strong." So David explained to Trevor what had happened. "I think I'll be going to court, well, maybe the policeman said. The lady said she was getting some man, I forgot what she called him; I'm getting sued or something."

"What's that?" asked Trevor.

"Dunno. My mom said I'm not to worry, it will be all right."

"Are you frightened?" asked Trevor.

"I am," said David. "I could get locked up. Anyway, Trev, come and have a look what the lady gave me. The box was so heavy I had to drag it."

"WOW!" said Trevor. "What was in it?"

"Come and see, you'll love it," David told him.

As Trevor walked into David's bedroom, with wide eyes and open mouth, he said, "She gave you all these for nothing? Yes, Dave, they are great. So now you have a train set."

"Yeah, I've always wanted one. I know it's clockwork and not electric like yours, but I love it, I will keep it for ever," said David with pleasure in his voice.

"Tell you what, bring your train set over to my house and I'll ask my mom if you can play with me in our loft and then you can run your train on my layout," suggested Trevor.

"Thanks, Trev, that would be great."

"I must ask my mom first though. She might say no as you know she doesn't like you, I don't know why."

"I know that," said David.

Trevor then spotted the boxes of soldiers. "Oh, soldiers!" he said. "I would love some. I'm going to ask my mom if I can have some soldiers for my birthday."

David felt good at that moment; he had something none of his friends had got, and Johnny will be green with envy, David was thinking.

"Trev, I think I'll show Johnny my soldiers."

"Good idea, Dave, he hasn't any of these and he'll be really jealous."

Off they went to Johnny's house and as they were about to knock on the door Johnny's mom opened it.

"Is John in?" they both asked. They couldn't call him Johnny because she used to tell them off.

"He's in the back garden. The back gate is open," she told them.

So round to the back garden they went and they crept up behind

Johnny. He was playing with his Dinky cars; he had made roadways and buildings out of bits of wood. He was making all the noises for car sounds, horns beeping, screaming of brakes and he never heard or saw David and Trevor creep in.

Trevor shouted, “Ah!” Johnny fell backwards, his face was full of shock.

“You idiots!” he shouted. “I saw you coming.”

“No you didn’t,” said David.

“Oh, yes I did,” replied Johnny.

“Anyway, Johnny, look what I’ve got, soldiers on horseback and a box of marching soldiers,” said David, proudly showing them off.

“Where did you get them from?” asked Johnny.

“My mom bought them for me,” David told him.

“LIAR! Your mom can’t afford to feed you so no way could she afford to buy soldiers,” Johnny said.

“She did,” David said as he turned to Trevor and winked, “didn’t she, Trev?”

“Yes,” replied Trevor. “I was there when she bought them.”

“I don’t believe you, either of you,” said Johnny.

“Where else would I get them from? You can see they are new. Well, do you want to see them or not?” asked David.

“Not really, I’ve seen them before in the shop window. Last week my mom asked me if I wanted any and I said no, I don’t like them. She’s buying me army vehicles instead,” said Johnny.

“Let’s go and play trains on my layout. You can bring your trains to run, Dave,” said Trevor.

“He hasn’t got a train set, you two are lying,” Johnny said to them both.

“Yes, he has, so there,” said Trevor.

“My dad’s making me a layout in my bedroom next week,” Johnny was telling them both.

Johnny’s sister was hanging out the washing and she heard what he had said and shouted, “You little liar, your dad’s not building anything in your bedroom and Mother isn’t buying you any toys.”

Johnny went as red as a beetroot.

"You've been warned about telling lies."

David and Trevor were laughing as they went through the back gate.

Trevor asked, "Why did you say your mom had bought you those soldiers?"

"Just to play him up because he's horrible to me. He always says horrible things to me. You don't, Trev, you're a good friend.

"Dave, go and get your train set, wind it up fully this time and let's see how far it will run on my layout. I'm sure my mom will let you in for a while."

"OK, Trev, I'll come straight back."

David picked up his train and ran over to Trevor's house, round to the back door, getting excited.

Trevor's mom opened the door and said, "Trevor can't come out again, he has to stay in."

David felt very hurt and downhearted. Why does everyone hate me? he thought. I've done nothing wrong. So off to his bedroom he went, laid out his circle of track, put his two coaches on, wound up the loco, coupled it up to the coaches and it did seven and a quarter runs round the circle.

After ten minutes he got out his Dinky cars. I'm very lucky to have all this, he thought to himself. He lay on his bed with his mind wandering. Boxing came into his mind. I wonder if I would be any good. I wonder where they train. I'll ask my teacher, I bet he'll know. Mind you, I do like playing football. I'm going to ask my teacher if I can play in the school team.

High Jump

The next morning when David got to school, he asked his teacher about boxing.

"Boxing? You? You're too skinny to box. Look at you – a good dinner would do you more good," said his teacher.

"Why, oh why, does everyone take the mick out of me, all I want to do is learn," he was saying to himself.

David's teacher then announced, "We have some boxing gloves; stay after school, some boys are training and you can have a go. Let's see how good you are."

After school David went into the assembly hall.

"So you decided to turn up?" the teacher said.

"Yes, sir, I want to learn how to box."

All the boys were high jumping, getting ready for the school sports.

"I'm sorry, sir, I thought you said tonight," said David apologising.

"That's right. Boys!" the teacher shouted. "Stop a moment, this boy wants to learn to box."

Everyone started to laugh, including the teacher.

"Have any of you boys ever done any boxing?"

"I have, sir, I've been boxing for two years," one boy said.

The teacher said, "Right, put these gloves on and show him the basic moves to start with and then the two of you can do three rounds. OK, off we go."

He pushed David forward, so all the boys made a circle and poor David just didn't know what to do for sure. Even though the boy gave him some tips on defence, he was hit so many times he just didn't know where he was. He was knocked to the ground many times and they where were all laughing at him again, even the teacher.

"Do you still want to be a boxer, you little ragamuffin?"

"Yes sir," replied David, but he was afraid to hit back, he remembered the bloody mess he'd made of that boys nose that got him into trouble, or so he thought it had.

"Try to dance round him and jab him with your left hand," said one of the boys.

"Well, David, you have courage, I'll say that for you," said the teacher.

David thought, this boy is enjoying hurting me so in the next round I'll run out and swing my right fist at him like I did to that horrible boy.

Out in the centre David went; he threw a right punch, caught the boy on the chin and knocked him to the floor, the boy was really stunned and all the noise and laughter stopped. The boy stood up with very shaky legs and walked out of the hall.

"My word, where on earth did you learn to punch like that?" asked his teacher.

"I dunno, sir," answered David.

"Come see me tomorrow and I'll give you the address of a boxing company. It's called Morris Commercials and they will train you up," advised his teacher.

"Sir, please, sir," David said as the teacher walked away. "Can I join the football team?"

"See me tomorrow. OK, boys, that's all for today," the teacher told them and off they all went to the changing room.

David walked over to the high jump stand; the bar was set at 5ft 2ins. He stood looking at it, lifting his right leg up and down. I wonder if I could do this high jumping, he was thinking to himself. He looked around to see if anyone was watching and then he walked backwards eight paces, had another quick look around to make sure no one was watching, ran up to the bar, jumped and to his surprise he cleared it. Phew! That was a good feeling, he thought. A good look round again, he ran and cleared the bar again.

What David didn't know was that a boy from his class who had been high jumping that day was walking past the hall from the playground side and he had seen David jumping over the bar at 5ft 2ins and had told the teacher.

The next day at school the sports teacher went up to David's teacher and said something to him. David's teacher shouted to David to go with the sports teacher. David wondered what was going on.

In the middle of the school grounds was a lawn and that was where the teacher took David. There, in the middle of the grass, was the high jump stands.

"Right, David, there in that box is a vest and a pair of shorts and a selection of pumps so sort yourself out a pair."

David tried on the pumps.

"They don't fit, sir," David told the teacher.

"Never mind go and get changed," the teacher told him.

David looked down at his feet, they were very dirty and his socks were full of holes, this made him panic, he ran into the toilets and washed each foot in the sink. That's better, he thought, I feel good now I've washed my feet.

As he walked back to the grassed area all the first-year pupils were sitting crossed legged on the grass in a large circle around the high jump stand, this time the bar was set at 5ft 4ins. David was losing his nerve at the sight of all the boys and girls sitting watching.

"Right, David, you are representing your colour group. You're in the blues group aren't you?"

"Yes, sir," David answered nervously, he was almost shaking.

"Good, the boy to beat is that boy there," the teacher told David.

The boy's name was John and he was 6ft 1in tall. David was only 4ft 2ins; the reds and the greens have been eliminated.

"Go and see if you can win the shield for your colour group, David."

David jumped and cleared the bar with ease, so did John. After a couple of jumps, John asked for the bar to be raised to 6ft. He failed the first jump and the second jump and so did David. Third and final jump. John jumped, the bar rattled bounced up and down but it never fell. David took a deep breath; the only sound was a bird singing in the distance. David stared at the bar and stared with all his nerves jumping. He ran and he ran fast and hurled himself into the air floating in the wind; he climbed and climbed with every muscle, screaming as he cleared the bar.

There came an almighty roar, all the children were chanting, "David! David! David!" even the teachers.

The headmaster sent a prefect round to every class to ask everyone to come and watch this little wonder boy. The whole school was now standing around the grassed area watching; it was a very exciting time for David.

Now the bar was raised another inch, David failed his first jump and so did John. David jumped over on his second jump; John failed but cleared it on his third jump. The bar was now 6ft 2ins. Both boys failed the first two jumps. On the third jump, John gave a very big scream as he jumped; the bar rattled, bounced, quivered, rolled round and round; everyone was holding their breath. David was willing it to fall and as the bar became less violent, it fell.

All you could hear from the crowd was, "Arr!"

Now was David's third jump, the silence was almost unbearable. Again David stared and stared at the bar and he was telling himself, I'm going to jump this, I am, I am, I need to, I need to, please God help me. Every muscle was again being stretched to its limits.

UP IN THE AIR, SCREAMING, COME ON! He felt the bar scrape his calf, it rattled and shook but it stayed on. The whole school went crazy; David had never known such praise, even the teachers were patting him on the back. What a wonderful time that was for David. The teacher even asked him if he would like a trial to play in goal for the school's football team. He'd become the school's best goalie, according to the headmaster.

After all the excitement had died down the teacher asked David if he had ever done any cross country running or any other running.

"No, sir, I've never done any running of any sort to do with sports," David told him.

“Right, next week it’s the area’s school sports. I want you to high jump for the school,” the teacher told David.

“Yes, sir!” David agreed, he could not believe what he was hearing, he had never been picked for anything before.

“This afternoon I want you to come to the sports field. I want to see what your running is like,” the teacher told him.

It turned out that at 100 yards he was fast, in the relay he was always the tape breaker and some years later he ran for Birchfield Harriers at Perry Barr. When jumping for the school against other schools, he came fourth but he was VERY HAPPY TO BE HIGH JUMP CHAMPION OF HIS SCHOOL.

The teacher gave David the address of the boxing company where he could be trained but he found that punching others wasn’t to his liking, especially when a smaller boy knocked him out.

Scruffy Boy

Back at school David soon realised that glory was short lived, because he couldn't read or write very well it was back to the bullying and the slapping on the back of the head and being ridiculed about his dirty appearance by the teachers. What he found to be one of the most humiliating things was to be stood up in front of the class and being told by the teacher "What a scruffy, dirty boy" he was.

David felt the only true friend he had was Trevor. By this time David and his friend Trevor had left school and were doing gardening. They had a big round going now: hedge cutting, digging, planting and taking rubbish to the tip for all their customers. David also started to work for a builder.

"I can't pay you but if you wish to learn the trade, I'll teach you," the builder told him.

"OH, YES PLEASE!" said David. I'll go for that, he thought.

"OK, tomorrow I have a brick-built shed to build with a tiled roof. I'll show you from start to finish how it's all done."

David was very keen to learn as in the past no one had ever taken much time to teach him anything. He became very good at all the building work and bricklaying; he loved plastering.

"You taught me well," he told the builder.

"Why don't you set up on your own and start your own company?" the builder suggested.

"No, I don't want that sort of responsibility," said David.

One Sunday as David was cycling round the country lanes, he spotted a sign on a board saying 'CREAM TEAS – Open 2pm–5pm'.

Looking at his watch the time was 4.30 pm. "I'm just in time," he said to himself.

The teas were being served in the hall next to the church, which dated back to the 17th century, David loved his old England. He sat down at one of the tables and was taking in all that he could; he looked at every piece of timber in detail.

As he was gazing a voice said, "Sir? Sir? Did you wish for tea?" It was the voice of a young girl,

"Er, yes. Oh, yes please," replied David as he looked up at the person who was speaking to him. What he saw was a beautiful young lady with dark eyes and black shiny hair, a lovely figure and a tiny slim waist. She was wearing a dark blue dress and a frilly white blouse.

"Would you like tea and cake, sir? I'm afraid I only have fruit cake left, sir," she told him.

David was so struck with her beauty he couldn't speak to her. She asked again.

"No—er—yes—I mean, can I is it?" The young lady smiled for she knew he had fallen in love with her.

"I'll bring you a pot of tea and a slice of cake," she told him.

"Oh, thank you." David was blushing even redder than a beetroot. He did notice she wasn't wearing any rings on here fingers and he was thinking, I hope she's single with no boyfriends.

"That will be two shillings please, sir." As he went to put his hand in his pocket to pay for the tea he caught the tray. Up it went – the tray smashed the cup, saucer and plate because he had knocked the tray out of the young lady's hand. As he pulled his hand out of his pocket very quickly, his loose change flew all over the floor. By this time he was a nervous wreck.

The young lady smiled. "Stop!" she shouted, in a soft but sort of stern voice. "It's all right, I'll see to it. Have you been here before, sir?" she asked him, hoping to put him at ease.

David was still apologising, when he finally came back to earth and regained some sort of composure.

"Call me Dave. No, it's the first time I've been down this lane," he told her.

"My name's Jean. It's nice to meet you. Why are you so nervous, David?" she asked him.

With a blush and a deep breath he found the courage he didn't know he had.

"It was when I looked at you. I fell in love with you," he told her, feeling very embarrassed saying it and still blushing.

"Thank you, David, that's very sweet of you to say that. I think you are a very nice looking young man," Jean told him.

"And you are a very beautiful lady," David was telling her.

"Thank you," she said sheepishly.

"May I help you to clear up?" David offered.

"That's very kind of you, I would like that," she told him.

After David had mopped the floor, he dried the dishes after Jean had washed them.

"That's it, all done. We've taken £25," she told him.

"What do you do with the money you raise?" David asked Jean.

"It goes towards a fund. We're raising money to repair the church steeple," she explained.

"May I help you next Sunday," David asked her.

"Yes, of course you can. We're having a jumble sale as well as doing the teas and we would really appreciate your help, David," Jean said gratefully.

"I have some items I could donate if you would like them. I'll bring them along," said David.

"Anything will be a help," said Jean cheerfully.

"OK then." Really fighting with himself, he plucked up the courage to say, "May I walk you home?"

"I am home. I live in the rectory, my dad is the vicar," Jean told the shocked-looking David.

"VICAR!" David said with surprise in his voice.

"Yes, are you shocked?" Jean asked.

"Yes—er—no, I'm just a little surprised that's all," said David.

"Does it matter to you that my dad is a vicar?" asked Jean.

"No, not at all," replied David.

"Good," said Jean. "I'm going round the houses on Wednesday collecting for the jumble sale, would you like to help? I'll start at 6.00 pm."

"Yes, I'll be glad to help," said David, "if it means being with you I would do anything."

"See you Wednesday, then," said Jean. "It'll be nice to be with you too."

"You most certainly will," replied David.

He felt so happy. As he was cycling home he kept saying to himself, "Why didn't I ask her to be my girl? I'm so stupid! Why, why? Damn it! Next time I'll ask her."
He talked to himself all the way home and most of the night until he fell asleep.

Wednesday came and David was very excited at the thought of seeing Jean, he just couldn't concentrate. He got on his bike, got of it and walked with it, stood on one pedal and scooted it; his stomach was so knotted it felt like a block of concrete. He walked into a shop and walked out again without buying anything. Started to walk home, got to his front gate and realised he had left his bike leaning against the shop window. David had it really bad, he was so far gone he made himself sick.

On the evening, he arrived at Jean's home at 5.00 pm. She had told him 6.00 pm. He was shaking with excitement; he walked up and down the lane where she lived. David checked his watch, it was 5.05, only five minutes had passed. He walked around the lanes again, it must be 6.00 pm now, he thought, checked his watch again – 5.09. He couldn't wait any longer. He went and knocked on the door.

As he stood there rehearsing his speech, the door slowly opened and there stood the vicar, Jean's dad. David was going all red and his throat dried up. He coughed and sounded like he had a sore throat.

The vicar smiled, "Have you come to see Jean?" he asked.

"Yes, sir. Please, sir, I mean," David said in a squeaky voice. The vicar smiled and chuckled a little.

"What did you say your name was?" asked Jean's dad.

"David, sir," he replied.

"Jean!" her dad shouted up the stairs. "David is here to see you. Come in, David," the Vicar said and showed him into the lounge.

David waited for 20 minutes. As she walked into the lounge David stood up, he couldn't believe his eyes, she was even more beautiful than when he last saw her. She glowed with perfection; he just couldn't take his eyes of her. Wide-eyed and open mouthed, he just stared at her.

"David," she said. "David. David, you are staring." David suddenly came back down to earth.

"I'm so sorry, you are so beautiful. I've never seen a girl as beautiful as you. God certainly made perfection when he made you." David hadn't noticed that Jean's dad had walked into the room.

"You are so right, David. She is perfection isn't she? The Good Lord really did smile on Jean's mother and I when he gave Jean to us."

As normal, David blushed from head to toe. "I do beg your pardon, sir," said David feeling very embarrassed at being overheard.

"It's all right, David. Have you come to help Jean with collecting for the jumble sale?" the vicar asked and told David to call him Donald. "Is it David or do you prefer Dave?" asked Donald.

"Don't mind, sir—er—Donald," David said in a muffled voice.

"Good, I'll leave you two to get on with things. It's very nice to meet you, David. I'll see you later," Donald said smiling.

"You too, sir, I mean, Donald."

"Thank you for the compliments, David, I felt really flattered," said Jean blushing.

"Oh! But, darling—I mean, Jean," said David feeling shocked at what he had said.

"Darling is OK, David," Jean answered, still feeling very flattered that David just kept getting struck dumb at her beauty.

"Come on, David, here's your ID badge. When you talk to the householders, show your badge and say you are collecting for the church," Jean told him.

David was surprised at how generous people were; clothes by the barrow load. The nicest surprise of the evening (well, the nicest was seeing Jean) was a Hornby train set in wonderful condition. It was an electric compound with two coaches and a 20-volt boxed controller, also in first class condition. His heart raced at the sight of these.

I wonder if I would be allowed to buy this set, he thought. Jean was over the other side of the road. David walked over to her.

"Jean, look what I've been given," David was so excited as he said it.

In a very calm voice, she said, "We've had these before, they do look nice in their box don't they? I think we have two coaches in boxes, or were they loose? I can't remember. I just know they are somewhere in the boxes at home. You've done very well, David."

When God smiles on a person, David thought, life does become wonderful.

"Jean darling, do you think your dad would allow me to buy this train set?" Oh, please say yes, David was thinking.

"Of course you can, David. That's why we were given them, to make money for the church. Do you still play with trains, David?" asked Jean.

"I haven't for a long time, but I will now," David told her.

It certainly had been a wonderful evening. When they returned to Jean's house, which, of course, was the vicarage, Jean's dad saw them coming down the path and he opened the door.

"My, you two have done well. A train set, good, we can always get a couple of pounds for those," said Jean's dad smiling,

"Sir, I mean, Donald, may I buy this train set, please?" asked David.

"Yes, David, you certainly can. £2 and it's yours," Jean's dad told him.

"I'll give you £5 for it. It will help the church funds won't it?" David said, smiling.

"It will indeed," replied Jean's father.

"Dad, did we have a couple of coaches left from the last jumble sale?" Jean enquired.

"I do believe we have. Excuse me for a moment, David, I'll have a look."

About six minutes later, Jean's dad returned with two boxed coaches, O gauge just like the boxed train set. "Are they any good to you, David?" he asked.

"Oh, yes!" said David with his eyes wide open.

"There you are, then, put them with the boxed set. The £5 you gave me will be enough for the lot," Donald told him.

"Oh, thank you," said David and when he looked inside, each box contained a green, mint southern coach, both made by Hornby.

"You look very happy, David," Jean's dad told him.

"Oh, I am. Jean, will—er—will you, I mean—" David was saying, stuttering.

"You're blushing again, David. What is it?" asked Jean.

"Will you—will you—?" David was saying, still stuttering.

"Just say it, David," Jean told him.

"Will you be my girl?" he could feel himself blushing again as he said it.

"David you are shaking. Yes, David, I will," she told him to his great delight.

David very gently took her in his arms and kissed her very passionately and told her, "I fell in love with you the first time I saw you."

"I did with you too, David," she told him.

"Oh, thank you, you have made me very happy." David was telling her and before he could say another word, she kissed him very softly.

On the way home David felt so happy he rode his bike from one side of the road to the other. He was well in love, one might say love sick. When he reached home he sat by the coal fire telling his mom all about Jean, how beautiful she was and how much he loved her.

"Have you bought her a bunch of flowers or a little token of your love? Ladies like that, son, it shows you care," his mom told him.

"I care, Mom, I care." David assured her.

"I can see that, son. I saw a lovely diamond on a gold chain necklace in a shop in town. I'll go to town tomorrow to see how much it is, how much money do you have saved?" she asked.

"I have £8, Mom," David told her.

"How much of that would you be willing to spend?" she asked.

“On Jean, all of it,” answered David.

“OK, David, give me the money and I’ll see what I can do for you,” said his mom.

David then went upstairs to look at his new train set, he was so happy with it he got the train out of the box and polished it on his shirt tail. When the circle of track was laid out on the floor, he put the coaches behind the loco and then it hit him – no electric points in the bedroom and there was only one socket in the living room. I don’t care, thought David, it’s beautiful and I’ll just sit here and look at it.

This is what he did. The only problem was that as he stared at the train his mind was taken passed the train and the image of Jean was there all the time. He got undressed and threw his clothes on the floor, as he had done all his life.

Life in David’s home was still very much at the bottom end of life. He got into bed and hugged his pillow, imagining it was Jean. It took him a very long time to go to sleep. When he did finally fall asleep, he was still hugging his pillow and as he slept he was dreaming he was on a tram and it was going downhill and it was shaking from side to side violently. He was holding on to Jean and she was shouting, “David! David!” He woke up sweating only to find it was his mom shaking him.

“David, David. You were dreaming out loud, son. I’m sorry, son, but as I ran into the room to see what all the screaming was about, I kicked your train set across the room,” said his mom.

“It’s OK, Mom. I’m sorry I woke you up.”

“It’s all right, son. You’ve taken me back to my young days when I first met your dad. If only it could last a lifetime, that feeling when you first fall in love,” his mom said and sighed.

“It will last for me, Mom,” David told her.

“Of course it will, son,” she said as she patted him on the head. “Goodnight, son.”

“Night, Mom.” As his head hit the pillow, he fell fast asleep.

Next morning David woke and sat up quickly, holding his head. He felt like he had never been to sleep. Poor man, he just could not think straight, it was love all right.

Suddenly he remembered his mom kicking his train set over. The loco and two coaches were fine but one southern coach had a tiny dent in the roof. That's all right, thought David, but I must be more careful where I use them and not leave them on the floor. He packed them up and put them in the airing cupboard with the others that the lady up the road had given him all that time ago when he had done the gardening for her. Every time he looked at the trains he remembered the boy whose nose he broke. I must find out where he lives, thought David, and apologise to him. I hope he doesn't hold that against me. He dressed himself and went downstairs and sat at the table for breakfast.

His mom asked, "Are you all right, son? That was a bad dream you had last night."

"I'm fine thanks, Mom. Yes, it was. We were, Jean and me that is, going down a hill very fast on a tram and it was shaking all over the place. That's when you woke me up," David told her.

"Oh dear, are those trains I kicked over all right? I'm sorry, son, I just didn't see them," apologised his mom.

"They are fine, Mom. It wasn't your fault, I should have put them away," said David blaming himself.

"I was wondering, son, would you like to bring Jean home to meet us all on Sunday for tea?" his mom cheerfully asked, as she had heard so much about David's new friend that she couldn't wait to meet her. She sounded such a nice young lady.

"Can't on Sundays, Mom. She does tea and cakes to raise funds for the church, another day maybe," David said to his mom as he was starting to worry about bringing his new girlfriend home.

"Our house isn't very posh. Everything is old and worn out. I can't bring her here," David said to his mom.

David's mom could see the worried look on his face. "Are you ashamed to bring her home, son? Because if she has been brought up properly, our poverty will not trouble her. She will only see people she loves."

David got out of his chair and put his arms around his mom. "I'm sorry, Mom. I'll bring her home tomorrow night if she is able to come."

"OK, son. I'll put the best tablecloth on and—" David's mom was saying as David interrupted her.

"No, Mom, lay the table as you always do, no different. I know Jean will love us for who we are." David agreed with what his mom had said.

David saw Jean on that evening. Her beauty stunned him every time he looked at her. He started to say, "Jean darling—"

"I love the way you call me darling. Your face expresses such passion and love," Jean said.

"My mom wants to meet you," David told her. Jean could see and feel how uneasy he was.

"David what's the matter?" Jean asked him, feeling very concerned that something was wrong.

"I come from a very poor background. My house is—" and David went very red as he was saying this.

Jean threw her arms round him saying, "Oh, my darling David, I don't care about things like that. I love you and of course I want to meet your family. I'm looking forward to it. Now come on and help me sort out all these things for the jumble sale."

After about an hour and a half David said, "I love being part of your life and all this. It makes me feel really good helping to do good."

"You are a good person. David. The Good Lord sent you to me so we can always do good for others," Jean told him.

"Yes, Jean. I'm going to dedicate my life to you and to helping others, that's the path I'm taking from now on," David told her.

"Yes, David, that's what we'll do together," said Jean and they embraced each other and kissed with a passion for life that neither had ever felt before.

The following evening Jean's father took Jean to David's house. His mom was wearing her pinny; it was stained and had been sewn across the pocket but it was clean and the best one she owned. She went out to meet them. Jean looked at her and threw her arms around her and kissed her cheek.

"It's wonderful to meet you. David has told me so much about you and your wonderful apple pies you make for him," Jean told her.

David's mom insisted that Jean's dad went in for a cup of tea. He was telling her he didn't wish to impose and, of course, his mom said, "Nonsense, our door is always open to everyone."

Jean's dad said, "You are very kind," as they were all invited to sit round the table and David's mom was pouring them all a cup of tea and cutting them all a piece of apple pie.

Jean loved it. This is the grass roots of life. There is so much love in this house, I love this family, she thought. They were all chatting as if they had all known each other for a very long time.

Jean said, "I'll wash up for you."

David's mom said, "Oh no, you are a guest."

Jean kissed her cheek and said, "I'm one of the family now." David's mom was so overcome at hearing those words that the tears were running down her face.

Jean's father said, "Yes, my dear, we're very happy to be part of your family."

After Jean and her father had left, David sat down by the fire.

"What do you think, Mom?"

"Isn't she so beautiful? She could be a model. She is so down to earth and so is her father. I might say the salt of the earth."

"They are, Mom, they are," said David.

David's mom said, "Look, David, your Uncle Bob works at the Carriage and Wagon Works."

"That's where Dad works isn't it?" enquired David.

"Yes, and your Uncle Bob is manager there. I'll ask your dad to ask him if he can help you find a job there. I know you love trains," his mom told him.

"Yeah, that would be good, Mom. I would be able to see how all the different parts are made."

That evening when David's dad walked in his mom said, "Jack, will you ask my brother, Bob, if he'll give David a job?"

"No. David is a big boy now, he can ask Bob himself," was his dad's reply.

"Oh, Dad, please," David was saying.

"No. You ask him yourself. Just tell him I sent you, here's the address," his dad was saying as he was scribbling it down on a scrap piece of paper.

I'll go tomorrow night, David thought. It's in the bag. He's my uncle, no problem.

So the next evening David went on two buses to find his Uncle Bob's house. I wonder what sort of job he will give me, he was thinking to himself. Being my uncle, I bet he'll give me an easy job. He'll look after me.

As he looked for the house number all these thoughts were going through his head. He won't know me as he hasn't seen me for years; I think the last time I was only four years old. I won't recognise him either, he was thinking, but when he knows I'm his nephew it will be all right.

David found the house and knocked on the door. His Uncle Bob opened it, he looked very surprised.

David said, "I'm sorry to trouble you. My dad said you might help me to get a job."

"Who's your dad?" his uncle asked.

"Jack, your sister's husband," said David.

"Sorry can't help you," and with that his uncle shut the door in David's face.

David never ever saw his uncle or aunt again, nor any of his children. Well, that didn't work, he thought.

When he told his dad he was shocked and told David, "You wait until I see him at work. I'll give him a piece of my mind," and David's mom hit the roof.

"My brother, well, he's no brother of mine. Can't even help his own. Shame on him."

"Not to worry, Mom, I still have my building work," David told her.

“I know that, son, but it’s no good in the winter is it?” his mom was saying.

David was agreeing, “Not really as when it’s raining they only give you wet pay, which is very little.”

The Jumble Sale

When the day came for the jumble sale, David worked with Jean and he just couldn't keep his eyes off her. A lady was saying, "Young man? Young man?" But David never heard a word.

Jean smiled at him and pointed to the lady. He looked round and to his surprise there were three ladies holding up garments.

"Young man, are you going to tell me how much this garment is?" one of them was saying.

David apologised, "Oh, I'm sorry, that one's sixpence. Everything is sixpence on this stall."

"That's cheap," the ladies were saying.

David told them they were keeping everything cheap so they would sell out, as it was all for the church funds. The ladies all agreed to pay a shilling for each garment.

"You are all so very kind," David told all the ladies.

Just then David spotted on another stall a thick album standing open. It was cigarette cards. He went over to have a look. There were three albums all full of sets of cigarette cards.

"How much are the cigarette cards, please?" David asked the lady on the stall.

"Two shillings and sixpence," she told him.

"May I buy them, please?" David asked.

"Yes, of course you can and they seem to be in good condition too," she told him.

He handed over the money and took them to his stall and put them behind his chair. At the end of the day most of the items had been sold.

Jean put her arms around him and told him, "You are wonderful and I love you so very much."

She was still hugging him as he whispered to her, "I love you with every fibre of my being," as he was gazing into her eyes.

"I see you bought some cigarette cards. The man who owned them will be pleased they have gone to a good home and that you will be looking after them," Jean told him. "I tell you what, we'll sit in the dining room with a cup of tea and look at your cigarette cards, these cards here are absolutely beautiful. These cards here with the birds on them have such vibrant colours and the gold edge really sets them off. I've just had an idea, David, shall we start to collect as many of these cigarette cards as we can find?" Jean was saying.

David agreed. "Shall we collect cards from one cigarette card company or all of them?" asked David.

"I think all of them to start with, and then we can choose a company that we like the best. We could have some leaflets printed and post them through all the doors in the area and we could even put an advert in the post office window," suggested Jean.

David agreed. "Now that's a great idea, Jean, I love you so very much. Do you really not mind me being so poor?" David was hugging her so tight she could hardly breathe.

"Of course, not silly. I love *you* not what possessions you have and not money. Do you think I am that sort of girl, then?" Jean asked.

David was feeling very sorry he had said such a thing. "Oh no, it's just that you are so pretty and you could if you wanted have the pick of any man on this planet."

"I have picked," said Jean. "I've picked you. Now don't you ever have any doubts again, you have no reason to be jealous."

"I'm very sorry, darling. I won't ever worry about losing you again," said David.

Jean reassured him, "Right, that's settled then." She kissed his lips so softly and with such tenderness that David went all weak and his nerves started to shake.

"When you shake like that, David, the love in your eyes shines out like sun rays from heaven," she told him.

"That's because I love you so very much," David told her.

"I know, darling. Listen, I'll still put an ad in the post office in the morning, but before I do that I must ask Dad if I can put our phone number on the ad," Jean told David.

David asked, "Do people have phones round here then? Where I live no one has a phone."

Jean told him, "Some do. Hang on a minute, I'll go and ask Dad about using our phone."

On returning to the dining room she heard David talking to himself. "I'll make Jean proud of me one day, I love her so much. I'll look after her and buy her a house."

So he wouldn't know she had heard him, she crept backwards a few paces gave a loud cough and walked into the dining room.

"Dad said he wouldn't mind but it might be better if we ask at the post office if they would allow us to ask people to leave their names and address at the post office and then we can go and see them," Jean explained to David.

"That's a great idea, Jean. You really are clever," David said to her.

"It wasn't my idea it was my dad's. Leave it to me and I'll sort it out tomorrow morning. No, actually just after dinner, it will be quiet then," Jean suggested.

David said, "I'll write out what we're looking for on pieces of paper and post them through all the houses where I live."

"OK, that's sorted. What if we also ask if they have any Dinky cars and trains?" said Jean.

"Oh, yeah," said David, then his face dropped. "I haven't enough money to buy lots of items."

"I've thought of that as well. We could sell some to fund what we wish to keep," said Jean.

"Who would we sell to?" asked David.

"Anyone. We could put an advert in the paper," said Jean. "I have £50 saved I'll use that to get us started."

"That's a good idea, Jean. You can have any money we make and that way we get what we want."

"No, David, we share equally."

"OK, but only after you get back what you put in of your own money," he told her.

"All right," Jean agreed.

Next morning David posted lots of leaflets all around his area, and Jean went to her post office at dinner time, just as they were closing.

"Shall I come back after dinner?" Jean asked.

"No, Jean," the lady said. "Come into the dining room and have lunch with us."

"Are you sure?" asked Jean.

"Of course I am. Come on through, we're having chips and corned beef. Is that all right, Jean?" asked the lady.

"Oh yes, that's fine. Thank you very much." said Jean gratefully.

After they had eaten, Jean explained what she wanted to do.

"That's no trouble, Jean, I'll put it in the window straight after dinner and I'll put any replies in this box here under the counter. That's all right isn't it, Father?" His wife always called him Father.

"For Jean that's no bother. If you call in on, say Monday and a Friday evening, you can pick up any replies. Is that all right, Jean?" suggested her husband, who she called Father. Jean had never known his name.

"Didn't you say you had some cigarette cards that were your granddad's, Father?" his wife enquired.

"That's right, I had forgotten about all those. Now where did I put them?" asked Father.

"I think they are in a shoe box, Father, on the top shelf in the long cupboard in the scullery," his wife told him.

"I'll just go and get them," and off he went.

Six minutes later he returned with a shoe box covered in dust.

"I haven't looked at these in many a year," he said as he blew the dust from the top of the box into the fire. He sat down, took the lid off and all the sets of cards were in the cigarette packets they were put in by the company. When you purchased the cigarettes one card would be put in each packet.

"They were your granddad's?" asked Jean.

"Yes," replied Father.

"Surely you don't want to part with them do you?" Jean said.

"My dear, they have been in this box for well longer than I care to remember. I've never even looked at them, I don't really like them," Father told her.

"How much do you want for them?" Jean asked him.

"You can have them with pleasure, Jean," Father told her.

That evening when David arrived at Jean's home, just as he was about to knock on the door Jean opened it. She threw her arms around him.

"Darling, it's so nice to see you. I've been longing to see you, I've missed you so much," and she kissed him with more passion than she had ever done before. David felt a warm feeling running all through his body. Boy I am lucky, he was thinking.

"I've a surprise for you come into the dining room. There you are, 42 sets of cards and all in perfect condition and in the original cigarette packets. These will start our little venture off," Jean told him, full of enthusiasm.

"Where on earth did you get all these from?" he asked with a surprised look on his face.

"Off the postmaster. They were his granddad's," Jean was telling him excitedly.

"How much did you pay for them?" Will I have enough money, David was thinking.

"Nothing, David. I even had lunch with them. After all, they have watched me grow up," Jean told him.

"You really are a wonder, Jean, you really are," he told her.

Some of the sets were in small amounts like 15 cards or 25 or 12 but most of them were in sets of 50 cards with pictures of trains, birds, flowers, places of interest, buildings, butterflies and famous people on them. Most of the sets had been given out by John Player; two sets were by Gallaher and Wills and one set of Churchman's and to David's surprise there were sets by a firm called Taddy. Those cards were very rare.

"I'll put my three albums with these and that makes a nice collection."

When David arrived home, his mom told him she'd had 14 people arrive with cigarette cards and two people with trains.

"One person left a box of cards for you to look at."

"Oh dear," said David.

"What's the matter?" his mom asked.

David said, "These cards aren't any good. It looks as if they were used as skimmers. I can see his address is in the box so I'll take them back after I've had my tea," but every time he sat down there was a knock on the door and by the end of the evening David had bought some 2,700 sets and 100 odd cards that could be used to make up sets.

By now all he had left was 14 shillings. One elderly lady asked if he would go round to her house as she couldn't carry anything.

"OK, Mrs—erm—"

"Just call me Dora."

"OK, Dora. I'll come round now if you want."

"David, ask the lady in. Where are your manners?" his mom shouted to him from the kitchen.

"Would you like a cup of tea, my dear?" asked his mother. "Please excuse my sons manners."

"Yes please, that's very kind of you. I don't go out much any more," said the lady.

"I do apologise, madam," David said.

"Thank you, son, you have been brought up well. It's nice to see young folk with good manners," the lady told David.

"How many sugars, my dear?" asked his mom.

"Just one, please," the lady replied.

After escorting the lady home, on reaching her house she opened the door and David saw four boxes on the table.

"There you are, son. Have a look through those boxes and see if there is anything you want," she told him.

At that moment David knew the Good Lord was watching over him. In the first box he could see a Hornby train set; it was a clockwork set with a 2710 loco with two coaches with red sides and a grey roof; one or two scratches but in nice condition. Under that box was a 2711 4-4-2 LMS black loco and tender in nice condition in a box – not the right box, but at least it was boxed and had been protected. The other two boxes were full of track, wagons and coaches, all in their original boxes. The fourth box had a station, signal box, lamps and signal and right at the bottom were seven albums of cigarette cards. I love it all, he thought, but can I afford it?

"How much do you want for the four boxes?" he asked the old lady.

"Nothing, son, I just want them out of the way. I've no children or grandchildren, my husband collected them and he's no longer with me so I thought it was time for me to part with them and he would be pleased to know they would be looked after," she told him.

David said, "Please let me pay you something for them."

The lady said, "OK then, have you got a young lady?"

"Oh yes, mam, and she's beautiful," David told the lady with pride.

"For payment, I would like you and your young lady to come to tea on Sunday. I don't have visitors these days," she told David.

"Oh dear, I'm sorry but I'm afraid Sundays are out of the question. She runs a tea room for the church every Sunday, her dad is the vicar there. Would Monday be all right?" asked David.

"Yes, of course it will. Seven o'clock Monday evening. You will come won't you?" the old lady said.

"Yes, mam. I won't let you down," David told the lady. He could only manage two of the boxes.

"Shall I come back tonight for those two boxes? David asked.

"No, make it tomorrow, son, I'm rather tired now," she told him. She was looking rather sleepy.

"OK, thank you very much," David said to the tired-looking elderly lady.

When he arrived home his mom told him two more people had been with cigarette cards.

"Mom, I can't believe how much stuff I'm being given, people are so kind. Look at all this, Mom, and I've only spent 14 shillings," David told his mom.

"How much stuff did the old lady have?" his mom asked.

"Four boxes. I've got to get the other two boxes tomorrow night.

She's very sweet, Mom. She wouldn't take any payment, I just had to agree to have tea with her on Monday evening and to take Jean with me as well. I can't wait to show Jean how well I've done. Thanks, Mom, for being a wonderful mother," David told his mom as he put an arm around her.

"I've done nothing," replied his mother.

"You have, Mom. You have allowed me to have all this in your house," David kissed his mom on the cheek.

Cigarette Cards

The next evening as David got to Jean's house. She ran up the path, threw her arms round him, kissed him with those warm soft lips and said, "I've missed you."

David held her tight and looked to heaven and said, "Thank you, Lord. Darling Jean, you should see what I've got and it only cost me 14 shillings. I've brought these few cigarette cards to show you but I also have a full train sets, coaches, wagons, a station signal box, lamps, signals and track points."

"You have done well. Wait until you see what I have," Jean told him as he was still hugging her.

"Oh yes, Jean, the elderly lady who gave me the four boxes of train items and seven albums of cigarette cards, she wouldn't take any money, she said we could have them for nothing but she asked me, well, told me, that in payment, would we go to tea on Sunday. It's all right, darling, I explained that you ran the tea room on a Sunday so she agreed we could go on Monday evening instead. Is that all right, Jean?" David asked.

"Of course it is, darling," agreed Jean.

"The lady said she never sees anyone any more. She lives alone and has no family at all. Thank you so much for agreeing to go," he said.

Jean asked, "Would you mind if I brought my dad along?"

"That would be great. I bet your dad will take her under his wing, he's such a thoughtful person," said David.

"That's why I asked," said Jean.

"How do you know he'll come? He may be busy," said David.

"He couldn't refuse to do God's work and that's how he'll see it. Talking about Dad, he wants to have a word with you," Jean told David.

David looked shocked.

"It's all right, don't look so worried, my darling. Come and see what I have."

As they entered the dining room there seemed to be what looked like thousands of cigarette cards.

"Wow! Jean, that's fantastic," gasped David.

"Yes, the postmaster had so many letters from the ad I put in the window that he thought he had better bring them to us. Because of the amount of people, well, mostly ladies, who even took boxes of cigarette cards to the postmaster and asked him if he would give them to me, he brought those as well as the letters," Jean told him.

"What a kind man. I must thank him," David said.

Jean's dad walked into the dining room where David and Jean were and remarked, "Isn't that a lot of cards, David?"

"Yes, Donald, people are so kind, aren't they? The Good Lord has certainly smiled on me since I met you and your wonderful daughter, you are a much-loved family," David told him.

"Thank you, you are so right. I do believe the Lord is guiding me and my family. David, may I have a word with you outside. See what you think, Jean is all for it. Let's walk down the path. See this little cottage? It belongs to the church and it's been empty for two years now. I know it needs a bit of renovation and seeing as you are a builder, I was thinking how would you like to rent it? It's six shillings and sixpence a week. As you can see it's a double-fronted cottage. The idea I had was that you could make one room into a shop and live in the rest as your home. I've spoken to Jean about it and she can't wait to help you clean it up."

Again David looked to the heavens and without speaking said, thank you God.

Jean's dad continued by saying, "And you will be very close to Jean."

"Sir, I love your daughter with every fibre of my being," said David absolutely beaming.

"I know that, David, everyone knows it. It's something you can't hide and she loves you the same way. All she talks about is how much she loves you and all she wishes to do is make you happy," Donald told him.

"Oh, Donald, she is so perfect," David told him.

"She certainly is," Donald replied. "Well, what do you think about the cottage?"

"I love the idea. I would love to rent it and I'll do it up for you," David told him.

"Splendid. Come on, let's tell Jean," Donald was very pleased as it took a worry off him as what to do with the cottage and it did need a little work to make it liveable.

As they walked into the dining room Jean was jumping up and down and raising her arms in the air. She was beside herself with excitement wondering if David would take on the cottage.

"He said he would take it, Jean," her dad told her, feeling quite relieved.

Jean jumped onto David, "Oh, Daddy, I love him so very much. I'll scrub it from top to bottom for you. I'll make it beautiful. Daddy, can we go in the cottage now and make some plans?" Jean pleaded.

"If David wants to then it's all right by me," said Jean's dad.

"You do want to don't you, David? You do, you do?" said Jean with a pleading look.

"Yes, I do," he really wanted to but how could he have refused Jean, the girl he loved so much.

So to the cottage they went. It was lit by oil lamps and as they made plans how to turn the room into a shop. Jean noticed a tear fall from David's cheek onto the floor.

"Oh, David. I know, you are so happy, aren't you?" she hugged him tight.

"Every day, Jean, I thank the Lord for sending you to me and every day he sends me more," once more he looked to the heavens. "I promise you, Lord, I will look after your angel until the day I die and I promise to always do your work."

Then David told Jean, "I will always do my best for you and look after you."

Jean told him, "I know the Lord sent you to me. That first time I saw you staring at me, I fell deeply in love with you, David."

"The same thing happened to me, Jean, you truly are perfection," he said, again hugging her tightly.

"Thank you," she replied.

"Look, Jean. I can put a partition here and create a hallway. That way I can use the front door as an entrance to the shop," he was explaining to her.

Jean agreed; she was so full of enthusiasm.

David suggested, "With a counter here and a row of shelves there, I can put some hooks in those exposed beams to hang items on near the wall, of course, so people don't walk into them. I'll start to plaster the shop part of the house first. Is that all right, Jean?"

"Yes, of course. I can't wait. I'm looking forward so much to this cottage looking pretty again," said Jean.

"If you don't mind, Jean, I would like to start preparing it tomorrow night ready for rewiring and plastering." He was telling her all his plans in every detail.

She said, "Mind you, I am so excited I want to do it all now, David, but I'm sure it's not possible."

"I can't now, darling, I haven't got my work clothes with me. Jean sweetheart, I think we had better tidy your dad's dining room up."

As they went into the house, Jean's dad was waiting for them.

"Have you two decided how you are going to do it?" he asked them.

"Yes," said David and with a pencil he drew the plans so Jean's dad could see and OK it all.

David told him, "I'll put a wicker fence around the cottage and a gate at the entrance and grow vegetables in the garden. I'll ask my brother to help me, is that all right?"

"Yes, that will be splendid. I'm going to sort some curtains out for you. I know our old housekeeper stored some away in the linen cupboard on the landing. Would you like to come and help, Jean, when David's gone home?" suggested her dad.

“I’m so happy, Jean,” said David smiling.

“So am I, David.” She kissed him and waved him off home and then she went to help her dad find the curtains for the cottage, she was so happy.

When he arrived home he told his mom all about the plans they had made.

“Son, that’s wonderful news, I am so pleased for you and Jean. She’s a wonderful girl.”

His brother was sitting on a chair by the fire and David asked him, “John, on Saturday would you help me with the garden and fence?”

“Of course I will, Dave, you know that,” answered his brother. They had always been close.

“But I had to ask didn’t I? I couldn’t just take it for granted that you would be free,” said David.

“I’ll come and help on Saturday too,” said his mom.

David told his mom that there was a bus there every hour. “Just find the church and the cottage is next door.”

“My family is surely blessed,” his mom said to him.

The next evening David cycled to the cottage with all his work clothes. Jean came running down to David just as she had before.

“I do miss you so when you leave every night. When you are living here I can be with you all the time,” Jean told him.

David said, “I will like that. I never want to go home and leave you.”

David suddenly realised Jean was wearing a jumpsuit and a turban.

“Have you been cleaning for me, darling?”

“I’ve been at it all day, and enjoyed every minute of it,” she told him.

David was so surprised. Jean had scrubbed the cottage from top to bottom.

“I can see you have worked very hard and it now smells lovely and fresh, like the scent of flowers. You are so good to me.”

Open For Business

Three weeks passed and David had plastered, rewired and finished all the shop fittings. Jean had arranged a wonderful lunch-come-teatime celebration. Unknown to David, his family were there and Jean's relations. It was a celebration to remember. All the toys and the cigarette cards were laid out in the little cottage shop and adverts were put in every shop window they could find.

Their shop was only open on a Saturday, not Sundays, as that day they both ran the tea room.

The first Saturday they opened, their first customer wanted some odd cards. These were two cards for a penny.

"We haven't sorted all the cards out yet," said David.

The old fellow said, "You do have a lot, don't you?"

As he looked around, pointing to the train sets, which looked like brand new sets to him, he said, "How much is that?"

"Seven shillings and sixpence. It's second hand, sir. In fact, everything in here is second hand," David told him.

"You should put a notice up saying that. Can I have a look at it? It looks brand new doesn't it? Would you take less?" the old gentleman said.

"I'll do it for seven shillings seeing as you're my first customer," David told him.

"Oh, OK. I'll take it," the old gentleman said. "I'll enjoy playing with this set. I had one just like this when I was a young man."

"Well, with the odd cards that will be seven shillings and four pence," David told him as he was wrapping up the train set in brown paper that the postmaster had given him.

"I'm glad I came now, I wasn't going to bother. I'll come again and buy some more sets of cigarette cards from you as you do have a good selection."

"Thank you, sir. Good morning," said David.

Jean came running over with a cup of tea for David. "Was that our first customer, darling?" she asked, feeling quite excited.

"Yes, darling, and I took seven shillings and four pence," he told her, looking triumphant.

Jean hugged David. "I know it's going to be all right, David, I just know it is," she told him.

That first day their takings were six pounds three shillings. David told Jean that they must put a sign up saying everything in this shop was second hand. As that first customer had pointed out, if it's second hand they must inform people of it.

Over the next few months Jean and David became proper little business people. They went from strength to strength and people from all over got to hear about the little cottage shop. They bought all sorts of toys and thousands of cigarette cards.

It was coming up to Christmas and Jean's dad said, "Look, David, Jean has asked me if I mind you opening up three days a week and seeing as it's Christmas, it's all right with me. Jean can run it on her own for two days and then both of you on Saturdays. I'm so proud of you both."

"Thank you, Donald, you're very kind."

"Well, it's all your idea really, Donald,"

"We're a team, my boy, a team."

"That's true," said David.

The three days worked very well and each day the takings were more than the day before.

A week before Christmas Jean ran up to David looking very excited.

"Guess what, David? I was just posting some parcels off and the postmaster and his wife asked me if I would like to rent half of their shop, you know, that side of the room off the main road shop area, where he always put our parcels?"

"I know, it's their store room," said David.

Jean said, "It was, but they don't use it anymore, it's just full of empty cardboard boxes and the postmaster, Mr Green, said there is a lovely bow window and he has an old counter in the shed. It's in a few pieces but it can soon be easily put back together, varnished or painted and it would be fine. He even has an old till in the shed we can have, anything he has that would be of use to us. He even has some old signs. He was very keen. What do you think, David?"

"Yes, that would be great. Is it all right if we go and see him this afternoon?" asked David.

"He said, yes, to go after closing time," Jean told David, who was so excited – a real shop with a proper till, he was saying to Jean.

"I know Mr and Mrs Green are lovely people and by the way the postmaster said to call him and his wife Tom and Pat," Jean told David.

"That's nice, Jean," and once again David looked to the heavens and thanked the Lord for all that he had been given.

Just about six o'clock, they knocked on the post office door. Tom opened it with a wonderful smile to greet them. He showed them round the room; it was quite large.

"I love that bow window," David said to Tom.

Jean was having a cup of tea with Pat, who had said, "Come on, Jean. Let's leave the men to talk business, I know we'll get the cleaning job."

"That's true," Jean agreed with her.

Tom was saying to David, "If you want, you could make a doorway next to that bow window or you could take this door off so people coming into the post office can just walk straight into here, that way it will look like one big shop and I can give you keys to the shop door. What do you think, David?" asked Tom.

"Keeping it as one shop would be better and we would never come back after closing time because after all these years you and you wife have been here self-contained, it just wouldn't be fair if after closing time you heard us moving about. But I must ask Jean what she thinks," David told Tom.

Tom told David he was very thoughtful to think of him and his wife and Jean agreed that keeping it all as one shop was the best idea and asked how much rent they would want.

Tom told them four shillings a week, "and I'll have the phone company give you a separate line so you can have your own phone number."

David said, "Our own phone, Jean. What about electric, Tom?"

"All in with the rent. You won't use much will you?" Tom told them.

Things were really looking up and two weeks later it was ready; counter and till, shelves and even cabinets that Tom had given them, and a phone now working. Over the entrance to their room David had fixed a sign that Pat had made: THE LITTLE COTTAGE SHOP.

Jean made aprons for herself and David; white ones embroidered with 'The Little Cottage Shop' across the top of them. It was a little slow for the first two or three weeks and as it was nearing Christmas again, the shop was packed with toys, all second hand, of course. The boxed sets of trains that were on show were looking like brand new and the rougher ones were hidden under the counter.

Jean put fairy lights up and a sign in the window saying: "MERRY CHRISMAS TO ALL OUR CUSTOMERS".

Tom and Pat loved the shop. They said it looked like all the items on show were new.

A week before Christmas a man walked in with 23 Triang mini vehicles, all boxed and in perfect condition.

"Would you give me £1 for these, please," he asked.

"Yes, I will," replied David.

"Thank you very much. They were my dad's and I can buy some food now," said the man.

David gave him the £1 and said. "Here, have this, five shillings extra."

"Thank you so very much. I see you also sell train sets," said the man.

"Yes, I buy them in too but they have to be in nice condition. Have you got any to sell then?" asked David.

"Only one but it's missing the tender," the man told him.

"Bring it in. I'll have a look at it," David suggested.

An hour later the man came back and Jean was serving.

"My, you are beautiful," he told her.

"Thank you," she answered, going a little red.

"I came in earlier and your husband said he might buy this loco off me." As she took it out of the box he said, "It's a Yorkshire."

"Very nice. Very nice box too. Have you the tender?" Jean asked.

"No, I did tell your husband it was missing," the man said.

"How much do you want for it?" Jean asked.

"I don't know," he replied.

"How about ten shillings?" suggested Jean.

"Could you make it 12 shillings, please?" he asked.

"All right, 12 shillings," agreed Jean. The man thanked her very much and off he went.

When David returned, Jean was laughing and said, "Hello, my husband."

"Ah, husband. I wish," he said dreamily.

"A gentleman just brought this in, a Yorkshire, and boxed," Jean told him.

"I've got a tender for that loco in the same condition but no box. How much did you pay him?"

"Husband," she said, smiling.

"What's going on?" he said to her.

Jean laughed, "He said he came in earlier and spoke to 'my husband'."

"I see," said David.

"I paid him 12 shillings," said Jean.

"Twelve shillings. That's a good price. I'll put it in the window," David told her.

As he said it a lady walked in and said, "I'm looking for a—Oh, I like this train, it looks new."

“It’s only just come into the shop, we haven’t tested it yet. We only sell second-hand goods, madam,” Jean told the lady.

“How much will it be when you have made sure it works properly?” the lady asked.

David told her, “It will be £3, but I haven’t a box for the tender.”

The lady looked surprised and said, “That’s dear, seeing how it has no box for the tender. I’ll give you £2 and how much are those Hornby speedboats?”

Jean said, “£2 will be fine for the Yorkshire, madam,” before David could say another word,

“The speedboats,” David told her, “are three shillings and sixpence but the loco won’t be ready until tomorrow. It’ll be oiled and tested for you.”

The lady said, “All right, I’ll have the speedboat and the locomotive. I’ll pay for it now and collect it tomorrow. Here you are, young lady, two pounds, three shillings and six pence,” and off she went.

That evening when they closed up Jean said, “I’ve got a surprise for you.” she took out of a bag from under the counter a Father Christmas suit. David laughed. “You’re to wear it every day until Christmas.”

“And what are you going to wear, may I ask?” he said, still laughing.

Jean held up a red dress trimmed with white fur all round the edges. “I’ll be wearing this,” she told him.

Later, David went along to see Donald, Jean’s father.

“Hello, David. How’s the shop doing?” he asked.

“It’s taken off really well. We took nearly £75 today,” David told him, beaming.

“Was there something you wanted to see me about, David?” asked Donald.

David now looked a little nervous. “Yes, I was wondering—I mean, do you—er—would you—”

“David,” Donald laughed, “now take a deep breath and say what it is you wish to ask me,”

“I’m sorry, Donald. Would you mind—er—would—”

"David, are you trying to ask me for my daughter's hand in marriage?" asked Donald.

"Yes, sir," said David, feeling relieved the question was out.

"Of course you have my permission. Have you asked her?" Donald enquired.

"No, not yet. I've been trying all day. I keep losing my nerve," David told him.

"Go to her. She's in the dining room now, my boy, and ask her," bade Donald, so off David went, nervously.

David went into the dining room, went straight down on one knee and said, "My darling, Jean, will you marry me?" he was shaking, hoping for the right answer,

"Yes, yes, yes!" she threw herself at David. He fell over and she landed on top of him, saying, "Yes, oh yes. I've been waiting so long to hear you say those words,"

Jean's dad walked in. He smiled and said, "I see he's asked you then."

Jean stood up, tears streaming down her face, saying, "Oh, Daddy, I'm so happy."

"So am I daughter, so am I," Donald kept repeating.

"I'll buy you an engagement ring," David promised.

Jean said, "I don't want an engagement ring, I just want to be married to you. When shall we get married? When? When?" Jean and David were so happy.

"I'll read the banns out for the next three Sundays and you can marry any time after that," Donald told them.

"Thank you, Daddy," said Jean hugging her father.

"Well, the quicker I get you married, the quicker you can start your lives together." I don't ever remember seeing two people so much in love, thought Jean's father.

"I'll leave you two alone now to start making your plans and I have my Sunday sermon to write," he told them.

"Will you come with me tomorrow to tell my mom the wonderful news that I am marrying the most wonderful woman in the world?" David asked Jean.

Jean said, "I'm the lucky one, my dad said so last week and we must tell Tom and Pat first thing in the morning."

As David saw a tear again running down Jean's face, he said, "I do so love you. I won't sleep tonight, my nerves won't stay still." All this time they were hugging each other.

"I definitely won't sleep either," said Jean. "I'm making plans as we speak."

The next morning they were both full of the joys of spring and they both went to the shop together to tell Tom and Pat their good news. As they walked in Tom was just opening up the post office.

"Is Pat around, Tom?" they asked in unison.

"Yes, she's in the back cooking breakfast, and you two look very pleased with yourselves," Tom told them both.

Jean said, "I'll just go and get her," and they both came back into the shop.

"Tom, Pat, Jean has just consented to be my wife," David told them both.

"I'm so pleased, you two are made for each other," said Pat, and Tom agreed,

"Congratulations, it's great news! We were only saying last week we wondered how long it would be. It really is good news," said Tom.

"We won't be doing anything in the shop today, Tom, we're going to tell my mom," David told him.

"That's all right. I'll sell anything that people want to buy," Tom told them. "And if I get busy Pat will stay in your shop."

"Everything is priced up and it's very kind of you to offer," said Jean.

"Go on now, off you go. You both enjoy your day with your mom," said Pat.

When they told David's mom she burst into tears at the news and started Jean off again.

She told Jean, "You are very welcome into our family, Jean. We all love you and thank you for making my David so happy. He wasn't really happy until he met you, he was like a lost soul, as if he was waiting for you to come along but didn't know it. We're poor but you are welcome to anything we have."

Jean told David's mom, "You are all so kind. You have the riches of the world of life."

"Right, David, you run up the road, get some cakes, spam and chips and I'll lay the table. We're going to celebrate my new daughter's happiness," David's mom told them as she got out her best tablecloth, which only ever came out on a Christmas Day and for weddings. Seeing as how it was only three days to Christmas and Jean and David were soon to be married, it was a most appropriate time to use the tablecloth.

"Are you going to live in that beautiful little cottage that your dad rented to David?" asked his mom.

"Yes, we thought that would be a good start for us and I can still help out at the church," Jean replied as they hugged each other.

David returned with the chips and cream cakes and said, "Mom, I've bought ham off the bone. I thought, only the best for my best girls," and then kissed them both.

David's mom said, "Best ham, this really is a day to remember and my favourite cream cakes – you remembered."

After they had eaten, David said, "You sit and chat and I'll wash up, Mom."

His mom was very pleased with the afternoon and told him to leave the tablecloth as she wanted to fold that up herself.

"I know, Mom, I wasn't going to touch your tablecloth," David told her.

Jean looked puzzled and David said, "It was Mom's granny's. It was passed to my mom from her mom and she treasures it and won't let anyone touch it," David told Jean.

"Well, it's the only thing I have ever owned that is decent. Plus it's all I've got that was my mother's," David's mom said as she gently folded the cloth.

Jean said, "That's nice isn't it, to keep something that your mother gave you?"

"Well, she didn't actually give it me but she always said, 'When I die, I want you to have the tablecloth,' so I inherited it. I will treasure it until I die and David, when *I* die I want you to make sure Jean gets this tablecloth," said his mom.

"I will, Mom, that's a promise," said David as he hugged her.

"Oh, thank you so much," said Jean and kissed David's mom's cheek.

David's mom said to Jean, "You can call me Mom, now."

"Thank you, Mom," said Jean smiling, it was along time since she'd said that word.

"That makes me feel good hearing you say that," said David's mom.

After spending a few hours with her new mother, Jean and David headed home and on the way they popped into the shop before they went to David's cottage.

Tom asked them both if they'd had a good day.

"It was a beautiful day," replied Jean.

Tom said, "I've taken £32 for you."

"Thank you, Tom. I'm sorry we left it to you," said David.

Tom replied with, "Think nothing of it, I really enjoyed it. It made a change from stamping books. Are either of you booked up for Boxing Day?"

"No," they both replied.

"That's good, you are both invited to lunch and evening tea. Is that all right?" asked Tom.

This time David answered for them both, "Yes, thank you. You're very kind."

"I'm glad because me and Pat have something to discuss with you," Tom told them.

They said their goodnights and walked home in the moonlight.

A Glass of Punch

Christmas Eve everyone seemed so happy. Tom, Pat, Jean and David were pulling crackers and throwing streamers and anyone who came into the shop had to put on a party hat and was invited to a glass of homemade punch that Pat and Jean had made. Pat had also made four dozen mince pies; a must at Christmas.

"This is the best Christmas I've ever had," said David.

"Me too," Jean said as she put her arm inside David's and held it very tight.

David then said, "Tom, Pat, I'll clean the shop up."

Jean added, "So will I."

"Oh no you won't. You're sitting down with me," Pat told them, "and we'll have a nice cup of tea."

"You three sit down. I'll clean it up, it won't take me long," shouted Tom.

The three of them went into the dining room and as Tom walked in he said to Pat, "I knew we had made the right decision."

"Yes," she replied.

Jean looked very puzzled at what they had said.

"What decision?" asked Jean.

"Oh, nothing," was Tom's reply as he looked at Pat and winked and smiled.

Boxing Day at 12.00 noon David and Jean walked to the post office. Tom and Pat were standing across the road from the post office; they were taking photographs of it.

“Hello, what are you two up to?” Jean and David asked.

“Just taking pictures of the post office. Do you know, David, all the years we have lived here I’ve never taken a photograph of it,” Tom told him.

“It would be a lovely photo to hang on the wall if you had it enlarged,” David suggested.

“That’s a very good idea, I never thought of that. The girls have gone in already so come on, David, dinner will be on the table and we’ll get told off if we don’t hurry,” Tom said as his eyes looked to the heavens, as much to say again.

Pat was saying, “Good job you two came back in, I was just about to call you,” Pat told them both.

“Told you, Dave,” Tom said as he looked at David and laughed.

David giggled.

“And what are you two grinning about, may I ask?” enquired Jean.

“I was just saying to David outside that we had better go in before we get told off,” replied Tom.

“Cheeky pair,” Pat said with a smile.

The table was laid out with more food than David had ever seen before; with silverware cutlery, Royal Albert china and napkins; a layout fit for a king.

After grace was said, the plates were handed round with turkey, roast beef and pork and four different types of vegetables: carrots, cabbage peas and runner beans. As they all started to eat, they started talking about the past.

David asked, “What did you do to get this wonderful lady of yours, Tom?”

Pat laughed as Tom said, “Our first meeting was a strange one. I was delivering a cow for my father to Pat’s farm and it was a very wet day. As you know, farms then had lots of mud everywhere and I backed the trailer with the cow in it up to the cow shed. Pat was standing behind the trailer and I didn’t notice her. Her dad shouted, ‘Pat keep your mind on what you are doing,’ and as she looked round, the trailer was right on top of her. As she jumped out of the way, she tripped and fell over. Well, as I said it was a wet day and Pat fell face down in the mud! I jumped off the tractor to see if she was all right and as she stood up all I could see were two beautiful blue eyes. She never said a word."

"No, because I was too embarrassed," said Pat.

"She got cleaned up, pushed me from behind and told me in future to look where I was going. I laughed and said, 'Sorry, you look much better now.' She started to laugh and then asked me in for a cup of tea and a piece of cake. We got talking, well, I did all the talking and Pat just listened very patiently. I remembered Charlie Prosser was to be having a barn dance on the Saturday evening a couple of weeks later so I asked, 'Are you going to Charlie's barn dance Saturday after next and are you going with anyone, or are you courting?' 'No, on both counts,' she said with a giggle."

"You don't half go on, Tom," Pat said as he related the story to Jean and David.

"So I said, 'May I take you,' and she said, 'Yes, thank you.' We had a wonderful evening, we kissed and cuddled," Tom told them.

Pat said, as she blushed, "Ah, that will do, Tom."

Tom said, "Well, it's true. We were very much in love like you two are now, and we still are. Anyway, that's how we met."

Jean, all dreamy eyed, said, "That's so nice and you two are still that much in love."

"We certainly are and I don't care who knows it," Pat proudly said.

"Everyone knows it round these parts," said Tom.

"You be quiet and pour the tea," Pat told Tom.

It was a very loving atmosphere that Boxing Day evening. Tom took Jean's hand and Pat held David's hand.

"You two are like a son and daughter to us," Tom told them.

Pat agreed. "Oh yes, you are. We love you both and we've talked this over between us and we have decided to retire this coming April. We have a lovely cottage in a beautiful village near Polperro in Cornwall. The decision we came to is that when you get married, as a wedding present we are giving you this building.

Jean jumped up in shock. She never said a word, she just fainted, but she came round after a few seconds. David was speechless.

When they got over the shock, Jean and David never stopped thanking Pat and Tom for ten minutes, who both said, "We have seen our solicitor and got everything done in readiness for the signing over of the property. We made it April as that will give us time to show you how everything is done and what to do. Of course, you have to see the GPO man to be passed."

"GPO?" said David.

And they all said at once, "General Post Office."

"Of course, it's me, I'm not thinking straight. There's so much happening all at once," David said.

Tom said, "The GPO man knows Jean and her father and told me there wouldn't be a problem making you the postmaster."

David thought to himself; that makes me feel good. He raised his eyes to the heavens and without speaking said, thank you Lord. David said, "I won't let you down."

"Tom, Pat, we won't let you down, ever," said Jean.

It was a wonderful cosy evening with logs burning on the open fire and Christmas carols on the radio.

As the time passed, Pat said, "I hope you still have an appetite, you two," looking at Jean and David. "I've made a trifle, a jelly and a Christmas cake and I've got some pears and peaches."

Jean said, "I'll help you lay the table."

"No, sweetheart, you're our guests. Tom and I will do it, won't we Tom?" said Pat beckoning to Tom.

Tom agreed, "We most certainly will."

When the table was laid with cakes, fruit, beef, pork, turkey, bread and butter, the jelly and trifle were put on the sideboard. Six beautiful candles were in silver candlesticks; there were crackers placed by the plates; all the silver ware was laid out; the candles were lit and the lights turned out; it was majestic.

The flickering of the log fire dancing on the ceiling and the glow from the candles was making the silver sparkle. David thought the dinner was fit for a king, but this is so romantic, I've never seen anything like this in my entire life. There was red and white wine also on the table.

David stood up, raised his glass and said, "God bless you both. May health, happiness and love be with you always. Jean and I love you very much and we thank you from the bottom of our hearts."

Pat and Jean both had tears running down there faces. Never could there have been more love in the world than the love that was in that little room in England at that moment in time.

A Job For Irene

January came and the sales were very slow but they bought in lots of trains and cigarette cards. In fact, David had a book with 72 names and addresses of people all wanting different sets of cigarette cards. Because he hadn't a big amount of money, he and Jean were offering less money for the items that were brought into the shop and he was refusing Dinky cars unless they were mint and boxed.

David talked it over with Jean about him giving up his job and running the shop full time after they had taken over the post office. Jean suggested that they could employ a young a school leaver to work in the post office. David told Jean he hadn't thought of that and it might be a good idea.

David said to her, "How do we go about employing someone? Have you someone in mind, Jean?"

"You know that little white cottage with the archway over the front gate with pretty roses? The one you said you liked so much?" Jean said.

"Yes, that really is a well-kept cottage," said David.

"Well, their daughter Irene left school at Christmas and needs a job. Her mother asked me yesterday if I could help and I said I would ask you. She's a bright girl, I've met her," Jean told David.

"That's fine by me. I'll leave all the hiring of staff to you," David told her.

With a smile, Jean said, "Good, I've given a schoolboy a Saturday afternoon job to keep the gardens nice and to burn the rubbish from 12.00 noon until 4.00 pm. I said we would pay him three shillings for the afternoon."

"OK, when did he ask you for the job?" asked David.

"This morning. His family are very poor and he lives in the next village," Jean told him.

"Very poor? Ah, that's fine, I know what that feels like. We'll take care of him," said David.

"That's for sure. I've seen Tom and he said it would be all right. I knew you would agree. I can't wait to marry you, David, that's all I can think about," Jean told him as she was hugging him tightly.

"All I can think about is calling you my wife. It's a wonderful feeling, my stomach is in knots," David told her as they stood in the middle of the shop in a sweet embrace.

Tom walked in and laughed and said, "OK you two love birds, we've got cakes and tea in the dining room." It's nice to see such love, thought Tom.

That evening as they walked home together, David asked, "By the way, what's the name of that young boy you gave the Saturday job to?"

"His name is Trevor. I did say to him that we couldn't let him help out until about the middle of April," Jean explained.

"Jean sweetheart, do you think if we ask Pat and Tom if they'd mind if we gave him the job from this Saturday if we paid the little fella? I don't want them to think I was trying to take over," David explained to Jean.

"I know what you mean, David. I would like to think we could help," said Jean.

"I'm really not sure. I really would like to help that family I'm sure. Did you say his name was Trevor? I'm sure Trevor would give his mom his earnings, well, some of it anyway. I used to give my mom some of my earnings and if she wouldn't take it I used to go and buy potatoes and onions or something like that, she couldn't refuse them," David told Jean.

"As a mother it must be very hard to take money off your children," said Jean.

David agreed, saying, "Yes, I suppose so, and they probably feel guilty like they have let you down. The frost is coming down and it's gone quite cold now, hasn't it Jean?"

"And Jack Frost will be on the windows in the morning. I love those patterns Jack Frost leaves on the windows; they sparkle if the sun happens to shine. So many colours. I love to see it, don't you, David?" asked Jean.

"Yes I do. Trouble is, when Jack Frost is on the windows it's bitter cold in my bedroom," David said shivering.

"Never mind, darling, it won't be much longer and then we can keep each other warm," said Jean, holding on to David's arm tightly. And he was thinking, what a lovely thought but he didn't answer as nothing of that nature had ever been spoken about.

"Ah, did I mention the other morning that when I woke up at 5.30 am I went to have a drink of water and the water was frozen in the glass? I couldn't believe it. I've never known that before," said David.

"Now that is cold," said Jean and David comforted her as she was shivering this time. They kissed goodnight and Jean went to the rectory and David to his little cottage. Boy, it's going to be cold in the cottage tonight. That's funny, he thought, I'm sure I just saw flickering flames through the curtains. As he entered the front door the warm air hit him. What a wonderful feeling when you are very cold, David was thinking. The fire was blazing away, the kettle was steaming on the Aga and there was a note on the table. The vicar had asked his cleaning lady to prepare some food for him, light a fire in the grate and light the Aga.

The note read, "The vicar asked me to light your fires and I've left a pot of stew in the Aga for you."

Well, thought David, my life is just perfect, I've never known such kindness. With my armchair by the fire, feet up on the fire grate, a bowl of stew in my hand and a big piece of crusty bread to dip in the stew and feeling very warm, life is just perfect. I must thank Donald in the morning for doing all this for me.

Feeling warm and very cosy his mind wandered back to his childhood. We were very poor but we were happy most of the time. My mom was clever, the things she used to cook with the very small amount of food and to make it go round all us lot. As he got warmer and more comfortable, he fell asleep with his feet still on the fire grate.

When he was woken up very quickly, his trousers were singeing and his legs felt as though they were on fire. He danced all round the room trying to cool his trousers down. He looked at the dish he'd had his stew in and it was in pieces on the floor. He felt awful, his mom had given him that dish so he went to bed feeling very guilty because he had broken his mom's dish.

After rubbing cream on his legs, he went to bed. He had a bad dream, woke up with a start and was shaking from head to foot. The dish he had broken had worried him and caused the bad dream. He reached for the glass of water only to find it was frozen. David started to laugh, his fingers were stuck to the glass it was that cold. As he looked at the clock he could see it was only 2.30 am. Out of bed he jumped and put his socks on as he hadn't any slippers. I'll get the fire going in the Aga, that will warm the house up, he thought. He could see the embers in the Aga were still glowing so he raked the ashes out, put a few sticks of wood on and piled the coal in. Yeah, he thought, it will be nice and warm when I get up again.

David was woken by a dog barking loudly, it was 5.45 am. Oh dear, thought David, I feel like I haven't been to bed. Brr, he shivered, it feels colder than when I got up earlier. When he looked into the kitchen, he could see the fire had gone out in the Aga. He cleared it all out and relayed the fire and got it going again. That'll soon warm up now, he thought as he got the frying pan out to fry two eggs for his breakfast. As he turned to get the bread, he noticed all the frost on the windows made the most wonderful patterns, he tried to scrape some off with his fingernail and couldn't, the ice was frozen solid. Oh well, I like it. It's Mother Nature wearing a new gown, his mom always told him that when he was a little boy.

With the fire now blazing away, eggs frying and David trying to toast two pieces of bread on a large toasting fork that the blacksmith had made for him for one shilling, he was now warming up nicely and the smell of the toast and the eggs frying made David feel very relaxed and comfortable with his life. He was definitely a very happy man.

A knock came at the door. Wondering who it could be so early, as he was opening it, a foot was pushing from the outside.

It was Jean. "Morning, darling. I've brought breakfast for us to have together."

David took the plates off her, placed them on the table, turned and put his arms around her and whispered in her ear, "I love you so much."

"Come on, while it's still hot. I've done us bacon, eggs, fried bread a sausage.

"It's two eggs now and a piece of toast each," David told her. "I've just cooked them, two fried eggs and a piece of toast each."

Jean said, "Lovely. I can't wait to be your wife. I'll spoil you every day."

"I'll look forward to that," said David smiling.

On the way to the shop the frost was so thick on the branches that it stood up about an inch and a half off every branch; it looked so beautiful. Jean went back to the vicarage to get her Brownie camera.

"I've seen frost on trees before but this is the best I've ever seen it," she told David.

"If they come out all right, do you think we could have them put on post cards?" asked Jean.

"What a great idea, Jean, you really are a wonder woman. Tell you what, I'll get one enlarged and hang it in the shop window," said David.

When they reached the shop, Tom was outside at the side of the shop with a blowtorch.

"What's up, Tom?" asked David.

Tom said, "Water pipes are frozen. It doesn't happen often. I think it must be quite a few degrees below freezing this morning."

David agreed, "I think it is, Tom."

Tom asked, "What's Jean up to with her camera?"

"She's photographing the shop and looking up and down the lane to get the trees in the picture with the shop. She wants to see if they would be good enough to put on postcards and sell them," David explained.

"That's a nice idea, I've never thought of doing that. She's a bright girl, David, you'll be fine with Jean," Tom told him.

"I know, I love her to bits, all she ever wants to do is please me," said David, simply glowing with pride.

"That's good, women are like that. Pat has always been like that with me and, of course, we men do our best to make them happy, don't we?" said Tom.

"Oh yes, we certainly do. No matter what Jean wants I go along with. I'm only living just to make that lady happy," said David.

"Here, David, keep the heat on the pipe, I'll go and see if it has thawed yet. I'll wrap it up in straw and make a box to go round it. I've been meaning to do it for years."

"I'll do that for you, Tom. You go inside and get warmed up," David told him.

Tom asked, "Would you like a cup of tea?"

Of course, David said, "Yes please."

"I'll make a good job of boxing in that pipe so it doesn't freeze again and then you won't ever have the problem when you take over the shop," said Tom.

Mom's Wedding Dress

The wedding day was only one week away. Jean had been to David's mom's for the afternoon and Mom asked Jean, "Where are you getting you wedding dress from? I've got some old dresses I'm going to cut up. I've got my wedding dress and I want you to have it. It's a little bit old fashioned I know but it can be altered to what you want it to look like," David's mom told her.

Jean was delighted and said, "Oh, Mom, that's a wonderful thing for you to do. Won't you miss it?" asked Jean.

"Miss it? I haven't looked at it since the day I got married. I'll get it now, you don't have to have it," David's mom told her.

When she held it up it was as white as the day it was made.

Jean said, "It's wonderful. Are you sure you don't mind me cutting it and altering it?"

"Not at all, girl, you do with it whatever you want," as David's mom was telling her, Jean hugged and kissed her.

Jean said, "Now I know what it's like to have a mother. You are so kind, only thinking of others."

When Jean arrived home she set to and altered the dress. It looked beautiful. Bridesmaids, she thought. My friend Pauline, we were very good friends all through school.

One evening when Pauline came to see her, Jean said, "I've got this lavender blue dress will it be all right? I can sew flowers on it."

So between the two of them they altered it and sewed the prettiest flowers and tiny bows on it. They both put their dresses on and the cleaning lady walked in and gasped.

"Oh my, you two do look so beautiful. Your David will fall in love with you all over again."

"Thank you. That's all right then, so all I need now is something blue," said Jean.

"I've got a very long blue ribbon and it will match my dress," said Pauline.

"I'll borrow Dad's old Bible and I've got new shoes," said Jean.

"What about bouquets?" asked Pauline.

"I'm going to make the bouquets out of God's creation – from the hedgerow – evergreen plants," Jean told her.

"What a lovely idea," said the cleaning lady as she dusted and polished the fire surround.

Jean said, "I'll put the blue ribbons on them and they'll be fine."

Next day at the shop Tom was talking to David about the wedding and asked him, "Have you bought your suit yet?"

"No, I was going to wear my black trousers and my blue jacket," David told Tom.

"I hope you won't be offended, David, but I have a blue serge suit, I've worn it only once and it just doesn't fit me anymore. If you want, you can have it," Tom told him.

"I could never be offended by you, all you ever mean is good. Thank you, Tom, I'll try it on."

David went into the back room and put the suit on. It just needed a tuck here and there.

Tom said, "There's a village three miles away, go to number 82 Hay Lane. The lady who lives there she is a seamstress."

With that, David took the suit over and the lady said she would be only too pleased to alter it for him as she had done alterations for Tom and Pat on many occasions. The lady marked the places where it needed altering and told him she would have it ready for the following evening and told him it would cost four shillings and sixpence, "But you don't have to pay me until you collect your suit," she said.

David said, "Here you are, six shillings. I am very grateful you are putting yourself out for me and I'll collect it at six o'clock tomorrow night."

When David arrived back at the shop, Tom asked, "How did you get on?"

"She's doing it special because I'm getting married and also because she knows you. Isn't she a lovely, kind lady? I'm to pick the suit up tomorrow night at six o'clock," David related to Tom.

Tom agreed, "She certainly is a very nice lady, David, and I can't wait to see you in it."

Tom shouted to his wife, who was in the kitchen.

"Pat, that lady who alters clothes is doing that suit for David. She is good. She has done some items for me hasn't she?" he was shouting all the time to Pat.

"Tom, Tom, I'm behind you. No need to shout. Yes, that suit does look good and she does a wonderful job."

All the flowers for the buttonholes were made of paper. They looked like carnations and they looked real enough.

The day had arrived when they were to walk down the isle. Everyone was saying how wonderful the day was and the bride was the most beautiful one they had ever seen and all the ladies and gentlemen who were looking at them agreed. The day was perfection; even the sun was shining bright.

David's mom stayed in David's and Jean's little cottage for three whole days. She felt like she was on holiday!

David and Jean got a taxi to the station and travelled by train. They arrived at Jean's aunt's on the south coast. David had never had a holiday before and to be away with Jean, his bride, surpassed all his expectations.

When they returned from this most memorable holiday Pat and Tom had left the post office and started their new retired life in Cornwall.

David opened the door to the shop, picked Jean up and carried her over the threshold. Then he carried the suitcases upstairs to the bedroom. He stood there in the doorway with his mouth open for a second or two and then he shouted, "Jean come and have a look!"

Jean ran upstairs. The bedroom had been completely redecorated and wardrobes had been built in wall to wall. There was a brand new bed with a full set of brand new bedclothes, a beautiful pink silk quilt and a bedside cabinet on either side of the bed with table lamps on, which lit to give a beautiful pink glow.

On the pillow lay a note, saying, "We hope you like the bedroom and in the envelope is a cheque for £2,000. We thought you could spend it on refurbishing the property as it may be a little old fashioned for you two."

"NO WAY! I love it just the way it is," said David."

The note continued, "We will come to see you both from time to time and we will keep in touch by post. I think we can remember the address HA! HA! God bless you both. All our love, Tom and Pat."

"I will keep this note till the day I die," remarked Jean as she picked it up and held it tight to her chest,

Again Jean was in floods of tears.

"I love those two people so much."

As she turned to look at her new husband, David said, "What wonderful people Tom and Pat are. Come on, Jean, I'll make you a cup of tea. I've had lots of ideas and I want to discuss them with you."

He put his arm round her they walked down the stairs very slowly. David guided her into the kitchen.

"I've got some ideas as well, David, I hope you are ready to do some changes to the shop rear," Jean was saying as David was making the tea.

"No problem, anything for you, darling," David told her.

As they sat by the fire Jean remarked how strange it was to be sitting in the dining room without Pat and Tom being there.

David agreed, "I know, I'm missing them already."

Suddenly Jean said, "This room where we're sitting now, I was thinking about turning it into a tea room. If you arch the doorway, partition the room off here and make a doorway there and put some cupboards with glass doors on them, we could display your trains in them.” She was pointing everywhere as she was saying it.

“What a good idea, Jean, and if I put a shelf up near the ceiling all round the room I could have a train running round it, that might encourage people to buy our train sets. I also thought, Jean, that if I put a doorway into the toy room on the back wall that would lead into the wash house and turn it into a mini museum with cupboards floor to ceiling, all glass doors and shelves. I could display all the very old toys that people bring in,” David said excitedly.

Jean said, “We could call it, ‘Days of Yore’,”

“Oh yes, Jean,” David said in an excited voice. “We two will never sit still!”

“We won’t, David, we most certainly won’t,” replied Jean.

The Post Office

Next morning Jean opened the shop and to her surprise, Irene was waiting outside the shop.

"Hello, Irene, have you been waiting long?"

"Good morning, Jean, only about 30 minutes," Irene replied.

"You silly girl, you should have knocked the door," Jean said with a smile.

Irene said, "Sorry, I didn't like to and I didn't want to be late on my first day."

Jean told her, "From now on you come round the back and knock on the back door."

All of that day, Jean was showing Irene how everything was done in the post office and told her, "When you are fully conversant with everything in the post office, you can work in the second-hand toy room and get to know all about that."

"Oh, I would like that, selling those toys."

David was busy altering the wash house and when anyone wanted to sell or buy any toys, David had to come in and serve them if Jean was busy serving customers in the post office, as she couldn't leave Irene on her own in the post office on her first day.

After a week had passed, Irene could just manage the post office very well on her own and Jean told her, "Just call me if you get stuck and I'll come over and help you out. Don't feel you are on your own."

David had concreted the floor and plastered the walls in the wash house and had knocked the doorway through from the shop to the wash house. After a fortnight he had completely finished the room; all the cupboards were in place and all lit up. He put a sheet over the doorway with the door open and made Jean and Irene stand and watch the grand opening, saying, "Unaccustomed as I am to speech making."

Jean said, "You do go on." Irene was laughing her head off at the spectacle that was unfolding before her.

David, speaking as he thought in a posh voice, said, "I now declare this museum open,"

Jean and Irene clapped. Irene commented, "It's beautiful. I love it."

Jean hugged David and whispered, "I love you so much."

"May I place all the old toys in the cabinets, please? Then I'll feel like I've done something for you," asked Irene.

"Of course you can, that's a lovely idea," said Jean.

David told Irene where to put what and in what cabinet, "But you can display them how you want," he said.

At the end of the day Jean and David looked into the museum and Jean remarked, "Oh, Irene, you have made a wonderful job of that, thank you. I like the way you've placed some of the toys on those paper doilies."

David said, "OK, Jean, now it's the tea room. I've been phoning the furniture shop about round tables and chairs. I've done some measuring up and I think we can get five tables in this room."

Jean said, "Well, I was thinking of putting a table for four there, a table for two there and there, and two tables for one over here."

David agreed, "Yes, Jean, that's a better idea. I'll start to put up those cupboards you want, I've already started to make them."

"Everything is going to be fine, David, don't look so worried," Jean told him, hugging him.

"By the way, Jean, I've put some adverts in the local newspaper to say what we've done and that we will be opening the tea room."

Jean was so excited.

"I can't wait, I think, darling, we will have to take on a young girl to help in the tea room if we get too busy. I know we will be all right, David," she reassured him again.

A Baby Girl

As the weeks passed the shop got quite busy but not that busy that they had to get more staff.

The first year was very fruitful in more ways than one. One evening after closing time, David sat down to dinner and Jean said, "Darling, I need to have the morning off tomorrow, I've to see a friend."

David said, "Of course, my sweet, you deserve some time off."

The next evening when they sat down to tea Jean asked, "David, are you all right?"

"Jean darling, I'm fine," David reassured her.

"Good. The old friend I went to see was the doctor and he confirmed that you are going to be a daddy," she told him smiling.

David's arms went vertical and he shouted very loudly at the top of his voice, "Yes! Yes!"

Then he held Jean in his arms. He hugged her and kissed her for nearly ten minutes.

"Here, you sit down, you must rest."

"Don't you start that, mister. Us women are strong. Don't you dare start pampering me," she said with a smile, "or I'll send you back to your mother's," David laughed.

The following five years passed very quickly. The baby they had was a beautiful little girl and they named her Wendy. On her first day at school, Wendy cried nearly all day. Jean felt so guilty and horrible for putting her little girl through such an ordeal.

"I don't want to go again, Mommy," said Wendy.

Jean told Wendy she had her favourite tea for her for when she was back home and little Wendy felt all right after that, mostly because she had made a new friend, a boy named Anthony.

He got hold of Wendy's hand and said, "Come and look at the toys the teacher just gave us to play with." Wendy ran off and forgot all about her mommy. Jean felt more at ease when that happened.

Just before she ran off with her new friend, Jean said to her, "Tomorrow when you come home, I've got a surprise for you."

Wendy asked, "What is it, Mommy? What is it, Mommy?"

"It's a surprise, you'll see tomorrow."

Next morning Wendy cried, "Please, Mommy, I don't want to go to school."

Jean reassured her, "It'll be all right, sweetheart, and don't forget I have a surprise for you when you get home," hugging her little girl as she was saying it.

On the afternoon when school was finished, Wendy came out all smiles and holding another child's hand.

"Hello, sweetheart, you look happy," said Jean, smiling as she greeted her little girl.

Wendy said, "I've got a new friend, Mommy."

"Oh good, what's her name?" asked Jean.

"It's a boy and his name is Billy. He only started today and he was crying 'Mommy' and I looked after him," Wendy told her mother.

"Well done, darling, you're so kind," Jean told her little girl, not feeling so guilty now her little girl was not so upset.

"Yes, he's nice, Mommy. I love him," said little Wendy.

Jean laughed, "You love him? Does he love you?"

"Oh yes, he told me," said the little girl to her mother.

Jean smiling said, "That's all right then."

Wendy asked, "What's my surprise, Mommy?"

Jean told her, "You'll see when you get home."

Jean had invited her own father and David's mother and father to tea. As Wendy walked in the house she saw through the open door her nanny and two granddads. Wendy ran in and jumped on her nan, hugged and kissed her and then did the same to her two granddads.

"David your daughter has a boyfriend," Jean told him, smiling.

"Wow, she hasn't wasted any time has she? Good for her," he said.

As they walked into the dining room Wendy was sitting at the table telling her nan and granddads that she had a boyfriend and how she took care of him. He was scared, she was telling them, because it was his first day at school.

"He's all right now, I told him I was frightened on my first day."

All the grown-ups listened intently and never said a word but Wendy talked non-stop all through tea.

After everyone had gone home and Wendy was asleep David said, "Jean, that cottage we had, I was wondering if the church people would sell it to us."

"Whatever for?" asked Jean.

"Well, I was thinking, my mom lives on her own, well, with Dad but no children left at home now and I was thinking, they both love it round here. I would do it up and they could live in it rent free," David explained.

"But there isn't any electricity in that cottage, David," Jean said.

"Well I rewired it didn't I, but I never got round to putting in the generator. I could build a shed, a brick shed, in the far corner of the garden, soundproof it and put a generator in it," David told her.

"Wouldn't it be too noisy?" enquired Jean.

"No, it would be all right at the bottom of the garden and as I said, it would be soundproofed. I think it would be OK. I could try it first, before I said anything to Mom about it."

Jean agreed, "I think that's a wonderful idea, David."

So David put all his plans in motion. With the church people, it took seven months to get a reply. The application was granted to them so David and Jean set to and converted the cottage. Even the lawn had been re-laid and a brand new fence put up.

"We'll put the cottage in Wendy's name so she'll always have somewhere to live in later years or she can use it as her little nest egg."

"That's a very good idea," remarked Jean, so that idea they both agreed on.

The generator was tested and not a sound could be heard from it and the cottage had been finished.

Come Sunday afternoon, off they went to see David's mom and dad. Mother was all for it but Dad wasn't sure.

Jean said, "I tell you what, you come down for a month treat it as a holiday."

"Well, I'll let you know. We're quite settled here," said David's dad.

"You might be but I'm not and I love that little cottage," said David's mom.

"Oh, all right for a month I'll give it a go," agreed his dad.

"There's a cosy little pub in the village, Dad. Remember you went in there a couple of times and you loved it?" David reminded his dad.

After a month had passed, David's dad was talking to Jean as they sat out in the garden.

"Do you know, Jean, I should have done this years ago. I love it here and Mother won't leave here now anyway," he told her.

"I knew you would like it and you have taken up gardening and you're growing all your own vegetables," Jean said to him.

"What I like most is being by you and little Wendy," said David's dad.

Jean was so touched by what he said that she kissed him on the cheek and said, "Oh, thank you. I must go now, Dada," she always called him Dada and he quite liked that.

The shop was now a big success.

The tea room only opened in the summer, but some ramblers asked, "Is your tea room open?" and Jean would make a special effort to accommodate them. Never turn trade away, was her motto. Everything was just perfect in the household of David, Jean and Wendy.

When it came to holidays they always went to Weston Super Mare. They stayed in a bed and breakfast where no teenagers were allowed to stay, only families. One year they took David's mom and dad, it was their first holiday ever and they loved it.

David drove there in his van with the sign-written sides: "DAVID AND JEAN'S LITTLE COTTAGE SHOP" and the address on the bottom of the sign. On the back doors were the words "WE BUY AND SELL TOYS, TRAINS, TEDDY BEARS, MECCANO, TRIANG AND MANY OTHER MAKES". David was surprised when people would stop him as he drove down the roads to say they had items to sell. He always told them to write to him with a list and his postal services grew and grew. Having their name on the sides of the van paid him dividends.

One evening Pat and Tom paid them a visit. They were so happy with all the changes that Jean and David had made and Jean insisted they stayed the week.

"It's wonderful to see our old shop, isn't it, Pat?" Tom said to his wife.

"I love the changes and it's brought trade to the area," Pat said. Everyone was so happy.

As the years passed Jean and David turned quite grey, Wendy married her Billy and they had two sons and named them David Thomas and Donald William.

The day eventually came then David and Jean did for Wendy and Billy what Pat and Tom did for them, they gave them the shop as an anniversary present and they retired to the south coast.

That little cottage shop was then passed on to Wendy's and Billy's sons when they themselves grew old.

As the years flew by, many people made a good living from that business known as "THE LITTLE COTTAGE SHOP".

THE END

Poem

A poem David wrote for Jean:

You are my dream come true, I will love you for ever.

The things I've said the things I've done
I meant them all every one
In my heart you will always be
You are my pride you are my joy
You are mine until the day I die
You are mine remember this
I've been in heaven since our first kiss.

To and for the prettiest girl in the world.

Two Little Urchins

Two Little Urchins

It was on a warm summer's evening one August in 1934, which was the year David and Trevor were born; the parents of both children were living in a two up and two down accommodation. David's parents had nine children already and could not afford another child with overcrowding poverty and his father not working; David should not have been born. Trevor was the child of his mother's eldest daughter, who was made pregnant by a fourteen year old boy – she was still a minor. Now Trevor was one of sixteen children in a two bedroom house and his future was no better than David's with so many in one house and always crying with hunger. Trevor was not wanted. David's mother was talking with the little girl's mother and she confided in her that she couldn't cope with another baby and was going to smother Trevor and make believe he died in his cot. "Babies always die this way, people call it cot death so no one would know what really happened," she said as she sobbed her heart out.

David's mother pleaded with her, "Please give him to me, I will raise him as my own."

So David then had a brother, a twin brother, or so he was told, and he believed that to be true for the rest of his life.

As they were growing up they were learning the art of surviving by any means they could: stealing, taking clothes from people's lines, taking bread in trays of twenty four from the co-op bakery where they made bread. They would take coats off hangers in the cafe and take them to the pawn shop; when the milk float was in their street delivering and the milkman was putting a bottle of milk down on a customer's doorstep, they would steal a couple of bottles of milk from the float; they even broke into the neighbours' gas and electric meters for the pennies they held. Around the back of the shops they found how to

I CAN'T COPE WITH ANOTHER BABY

pick the locks to greengrocers and steal the apples, oranges, bananas, and from the butchers joints of meat – each and every way to help feed their brothers and sisters, but they were heading for a big fall if they ever got caught.

David and Trevor lived rough as there wasn't any room in their house. They ate by finding a place to sit down wherever they could. They both lived in the wash house at the bottom of the yard, also known as the brew house; it was around six or seven square feet. In the wash house there was a large brick built boiler; when one of the women did the washing and lit the boiler to boil the clothes on their allocated washing day, it was very warm by night time from the fire that had been alight to heat the water for the washing. If Trevor and David's clothes had got wet in the rain or snow that day they could always dry off their clothes so they were ready for the next day. Their beds were just old ticks which were full of holes, but filled with straw they were very comfortable and they soon became very warm. During the night sometimes scurrying mice or even a rat peering through the gap under the door would wake them. They did not have such luxury as a blanket but they made do with some old coats and a bit of old rug just to keep themselves covered – they didn't even possess a pillow, all they had was screwed up straw with a piece of rag to cover over it. They never felt worried about having to sleep in the wash house as all the neighbours knew of their situation and they accepted it was the boys' bedroom as there were twenty or more who all shared the facilities available. Toilets, washhouse, even the clothes line was shared, and they all looked after each other as true loving Christians do. All the Toilets were in blocks of six – three back to back in small rows; all of these had old fashioned bench sheets with overhead flush systems and each toilet was shared by two families. Toilet paper was nonexistent – only small squares of newspaper threaded onto a piece of string that was hung on a nail that had been knocked into the mortar joint on the toilet wall. With so many children in each family there was usually a queue for the toilet. These toilet blocks were several yards from the house, so in cold weather it would be very uncomfortable walking to the toilet, but sleeping in the wash house had its compensations. The boys could wake up early with the men going off to work, which meant David and Trevor would be up to use the toilets before all of the other households were up. They took their tin drum to empty down the toilet (the boys never had a bucket only a gallon tin drum they had found on the tip) and if there was any wood left from the day before the boys, would light the fire under the copper after they had filled it up with water ready for whoever was going to do their washing that day.

The women had a rota for which mother was going to use the wash house for their washing day. The boys always helped the mothers, trying to make life a little easier for them. Sometimes they would get the fire ready the night before. They would put water in the copper and get the fire ready with wood that was once part of a fence that went around their little garden outside the wash house. Just before they went to sleep, if it was cold and they had plenty of wood they would light the fire to boil the water so they could wash the next morning in warm water. Using old stockings that were their moms', they filled them with dried grass and these were used to stop the draft from the top and bottom of the door. There was a window to let daylight in but this did not open; a sack they had stolen from the back of the greengrocers was placed over the window, and there were two nails that were used for the purpose of hanging the sack to keep out the daylight rather than opening the door and losing all the heat. When they needed the toilet, which was only two yards from where they were, they used the old tin drum they had found on the tip. Their mother and father had a bucket which was emptied every morning by one of the children. When their brothers and sisters needed the toilet at night they tiptoed into the parents' bedroom to use the bucket.

There was a chore list on the wall in the kitchen to say who was to do what that morning. After having a wash they got ready for school and their mom gave them one slice of toast to eat on their way to school and one to eat at break time; they didn't have anything but water to drink, they were used to that as it happened every morning. On rare occasions they had a saucer of porridge and a saucer of milk; the milk was poured onto the same saucer that the porridge had been on as they only had two cups in that household.

On the way out of the gate David caught his trousers on a nail; it ripped a hole in the back of them. “Trev,” David shouted, “I will catch you up.” As David got back into the house he told his mother that he had ripped his trousers.

“Oh dear, I haven’t any grey material, this will have to do,” said his mother, as she hung up a red piece of material whilst David was still in his short trousers.

“Oh, Mom, not red!”

“This is all I have, it will do for now. I will ask Mrs Kendal if she has a piece of grey – if she has, then I can change it tonight.”

David knew he was in for some micky taking at school. As he was late for assembly he was told to wait outside the headmaster’s office, so he tried to smarten himself up as he knew the headmaster would shout at him for looking so scruffy. But not only did he shout at him, he gave him the cane as well.

David had to go to the examination room straight after leaving the headmaster’s office, as his class had a medical that morning. After assembly all the boys were lining up waiting for their turn to be examined.

The teacher shouted, as he always did, “Strip down to your underpants.” Everyone stripped, but David left his trousers on – he hadn’t any underwear; he hadn’t had any since the day he was born.

As the teacher walked down the line of boys inspecting, when he came down to David he said, “Strip down to your underpants.”

In a very soft voice David said, “Please, Sir, I haven’t any underpants.”

“What? No underpants?” he shouted. “What is this red patch in your trousers?” He had David by the arm and was shaking him very violently. “You are a disgrace! Look at your feet. When you get home have a bath; I suppose you will bath in a puddle you disgusting little boy.”

All the boys were giggling. David thought to himself, when I’m older I’m going to get him, I will beat him up.

When the bell went for playtime he went and stood in the corner of the playground with his back to the fence so the red patch could not be seen.

TREV IM GOING OUT TO THE COUNTRYSIDE TOMORROW
TO FIND SOME NEW CLOTHES GOOD IDEA DAVE NITE.

Trevor walked up to him and said, "What's up Dave, you look upset?"

"That rotten teacher was taking the mick, and all the boys were laughing at me."

"Who was laughing the most?"

"Him, that Tony; let's get him."

"Ok."

Trevor walked up to Tony and punched him on the nose. "Laugh at my brother, will you?"

As he punched him again David ran up to Tony and kicked him as hard as he could in the face. Tony's nose split wide open. All the boys were around in circle shouting, "Fight! Fight!"

The teacher on playground duty was blowing his whistle, grabbed David and Trevor by the hair and swung them around. They went flying across the playground and Trevor cut his knee. Tony was picked up and carried off; he was off school for three weeks. The headmaster had both David and Trevor in his office. He was in a rage – as he was screaming at them and slapping their faces very hard.

"Bend over the desk," he commanded. He gave them both six strokes of the cane. As he opened the door he ordered them out and slapped them on the back of the head. "Now go back to your classroom."

Feeling very shaky and in pain, David said, "Trev, I'm going home."

"That's a good idea, Dave," replied Trevor. So they both ran out of the school gates.

Feeling hungry, they went to the back of the greengrocers where they had been many times before. Trevor kept watch out and when the coast was clear David stole some bananas, apples and a couple of oranges and then off they ran together.

"Dave, let's go to the tip, no one will see us there." said Trevor.

On the way to the tip they saw the baker delivering the bread door to door.

"Dave, you keep him talking whilst I nick a loaf."

"Ok, Trev, I will stroke the horse and talk to the baker."

Trevor stuffed the loaf up his shirt and then he ran as fast as he could just in case he was spotted. David went to the tip where his brother was waiting, already filling his face with the bread. They sat down on an old log, the bread and bananas tasted very sweet. At the far corner of the tip were lots of brambles and a big oak tree. Whilst they were exploring, they found that behind the oak tree, where all the brambles were really dense, they could get inside the brambles; it looked just like a room. "Trev, we will have this as our den," David said in an excited voice. With old corrugated tin sheets they found on the tip, they lined the inside of the den so the brambles would not scratch them. The time was getting on so they started heading home with armfuls of firewood for the copper.

In the washhouse, Trevor said, "I will give Mom one of the apples and this orange. We can have half of this apple each and I will get her some more tomorrow."

With a gasp David said, "Look at our clothes, we have got them all dirty." They got the ashes out from under the copper and with small pieces of lino David placed them in between the wood and pieces of paper. He tried to light the fire under the copper but the wood was a little damp, it kept going out. It took four attempts before the fire was finally alight. Their shirts were thrown into the copper and after they had boiled them for half an hour or so they took them out and they were sort of clean, a little better than before anyway.

Next morning, David said to his brother, "Trev, I'm not going to school today."

"If you're not, then I'm not neither," replied Trevor.

They played truant from school for two weeks. Their mom did not know that they were not going to school – well not until the School Board man went to see why they had not been to school for the past two weeks. Their mom realised what they had been up to very quickly, so she told the School Board man that they both had measles and should be back to school in a few days time.

When they both returned from the tip making believe they had just come home from school, she made them a plate of stew and asked if they had enjoyed their day at school. Trevor answered with a no, saying he hated school, whilst David was agreeing with what Trevor had said.

THE WASH HOUSE WHERE DAVID AND TREVOR SLEEPS.

"Haven't I told you to never lie to me?" she said whilst she caned them both for lying. As she hung the cane back on the nail at the side of the fireplace, she ordered them to go into the wash house and stay there until she told them to leave; they would not dare defy their mother.

Many people in their area kept chickens, so they soon learnt how, where and when to get eggs, they even took a chicken when food was really in short supply – rationing made most families go hungry. David and Trevor were really on their own when it came to surviving; one could say that the poorest family in the road were fed the best, thanks to David and Trevor's dishonesty.

As time passed, peace in the world was being turned into trouble because a horrible man in Germany was upsetting everyone – well everyone in England at that time; it was now 1941. David and Trevor were now seven years old and having to live and survive the way they always had. They came across as much older than they really were. By this time their dad was in the army. As most of the young men were called up to do their duty for the country with all the men at war, it meant there were Saturday jobs that young boys were able to get. David got a job at the greengrocers, which was called Browns, the same greengrocers that they had stolen from many times before. Stealing from there now would be much easier; he would get an old box and fill it with fruit when it was available. Potatoes and other vegetables seemed to be plentiful at that moment in time. The box was placed outside the back gates under a pile of old boxes that were stained from the fruit, then Trevor would collect it and take it home.

A few weeks after Trevor had got himself a Saturday job at a grocery shop called Wrenson's, he was taught how to weigh the tea into quarters of a pound, even 2ounces. He would pour the tea from the scoop into little blue bags. Sugar was weighed in 1 pound bags, half pounds and 2ounces, which he also put into the blue bags. He could not read or write but very quickly he had learnt about the grocery trade. Trevor had also learnt how to smuggle out items of groceries for his mom. Between them, David and Trevor were feeding their brothers and sisters every week. Two of their older brothers were also called up to do their duty, so the burden on their mother was decreased.

CORR LOOK DAVE PEARLS.

David and Trevor still had to sleep in the wash house. At their Saturday jobs they were both given a shilling; they kept sixpence and gave their mom sixpence. She loved them so much, one day she made a whole apple pie for them to eat to themselves.

David had saved up all of his sixpences and bought himself a brand new pair of pumps. What joy he thought, I can now walk in the rain without getting my feet wet. Trevor had also been saving his sixpences but he had bought saving stamps from the post office and stuck them in a book that was supplied free when you bought the stamps.

All was going well for both of them. They both decided to start looting the bombed houses. David got a wonderful Hornby train set from one of the bombed out houses, and Trevor found a tin full of lead soldiers, so for a short while they both went back to the wash house and played with their new-found toys and finally became children again, except it only lasted for a couple of hours, but at least they did find childhood enjoyable. They both agreed that the next day the both of them would go out and try to find some more toys to play with.

The next day they walked to school and as they approached the school gates they got a shock – they saw it had been bombed and burnt down to the ground. They were so excited – that was the only excuse they needed to never go to school again, well not whilst the war was on anyway. So from then on looting and stealing became even bigger in their young lives, in fact they considered it to be fine to steal and loot – their brothers and sisters lived better when they did.

One evening after a bomb raid, a clothes shop had been bombed so David and Trevor ran into the shop, got two pairs of trousers for themselves and a coat for Mom but an air raid warden had caught them so he started shouting at them and saying they could get locked up – at worst even shot. Luckily, they were so good at lying that they convinced the warden that the owner was at the back of the shop and they were just helping him. Puzzled, the warden went to look and Trevor and David took their chance to run; they were so fast they were out of sight in seconds. When they reached home they gave their mom the coat that they had stolen, but she was confused as to where they had got it from. They lied to her and told her that the coat was blown onto the rubble, it belonged to no one. Their mother loved it, she hadn't had anything new for years so she tried it on but it was too small.

"That's not the right size, is it Mom?" David said.

"Oh well," she said, in a very disappointed voice, "I can sell it."

Trevor told David that they could go back to the shop where they got the coat from and get one for their mom that fitted her. So off they went to start looting again – they knew no fear at all. When they reached the shop they had looted, to their horror, the owners were there cleaning up and checking the stock to see what was ruined or missing. There was glass dust and rubble everywhere.

"Can we help you, mister?" Trevor asked.

"Ok lads, you can help to clear all this glass up."

They worked hard but there wasn't any way that they could get their hands on any of the goods, which meant they had to look elsewhere for a coat for their mom. After they had finished helping to clean the shop they got sixpence each – they were very happy with that as money was hard to get in those hard times.

That night there was very heavy bombing. Fortunately it was a little way off from their street, but the next morning mom told them that their nan's house had been hit; lucky enough she was ok, but the house wasn't, which meant she had to come and stay with them, so she agreed she would spend the nights with David and Trevor in the wash house. She preferred this anyway as she couldn't stand the thought of being in a house again whilst bombs were being dropped everywhere. Nan was a very upright lady with very strong morals and did not like the idea of Mom having so many children; never the less she still helped her out. Every weekend two of the girls in the family would go to Nan's and stop there, which would give Mom a break. That now, of course, was impossible as Nan's house had been bombed. Their granddad had died a few years before the war started due to pneumonia and bronchitis; he was always ill in the later years of his life, so when the girls did go to Nan's it would be good company for her. Their mom did have a sister but she was killed at the beginning of the war and her children had gone to live with their dad. The thought of Nan sharing the night in the wash house with Dave and Trevor gave them the creeps because of her being so strict, especially with the boys in the family. This meant things were about to change, but it was not for the worst because they knew she would give them that extra bit of care, which is what they needed at the time. Or so they thought.

The very first morning David and Trevor went out and Nan had gone back into the house after sleeping in an old chair. David and Trevor had gone out looking for new bombed buildings, there were many of these to explore and loot to make some money. They found a bundle of clothes for the pawn shop and a couple of blankets for Mom; lumps of coal for the fire, anything that Dave and Trevor thought would be useful for Mom went home with them – buckets, bowls, anything. They put all their looted goods under the stairs, and then in walked Nan, who realised what they had been doing and gave them both a good telling off, saying that the poor people who were bombed would be coming back to claim their goods, and that they were nothing but common thieves and she was going to change them.

"Oh Nan, don't shout at me, we are only doing this for you," Trevor said.

David walked in with a big smile. "Look what I have got for you, it is a bed chair and I have found a really soft mattress."

Well, Nan, who normally was moral and upstanding, said, "Oh well, erm erm, that's very thoughtful of you, where did you get that from?"

"A lady gave it to me. I told her my Nan had been bombed so she was coming to live with us but she hadn't a bed to sleep on."

Trevor glared at David as Nan was pushing her hands into the mattress. David shrugged his shoulders and mouthed silently to Trevor that he did not know what else he could say.

"It will be ok for now," Nan sighed. "Thank you boys, I know you meant well but I will have no more of this looting and stealing."

"We don't, Nan," the boys said at the same time.

"I am not stupid," she replied. "Right boys, we will start as we mean to go on, get the mop and bucket, you two are going to scrub the place clean." The look of horror grew on the two boys' faces as she pushed them out of the wash house. "Go and get a scrubbing brush and a bucket."

David and Trevor went to ask their mother if she had a scrubbing brush. David looked at Trevor as they walked slowly towards the house. "Let's tell her Mom ain't got a scrubbing brush. I'm going to sleep in our den whilst Nan is here, we will be moaned at from morning until night. We will have to hide all of our looted finds in our den," said David.

"Come on, boys, come on, we have a lot to do."

Just at that moment, Mother called, saying she had done a cup of tea.

"Right boys, get this place cleaned up by the time I get back."

David and Trevor did not like the idea of this so they decided to take off.

"I am going to look around the bombed houses to see if we can find any furniture for our den; I'm not staying in that wash house with her."

"You mean Nan," Trevor said.

"Yeah, Nan," replied Dave.

So round the bombed houses they went but they were chased and caught by the air raid warden. He gave them a real good shaking, telling them he was going to take them to the police station. Just as the warden had said 'station' Trevor gave him such a kick in the shin he let go of the boys' arms, so they ran like the wind. The warden was angrily shouting all kinds of abuse at them as they disappeared around the corner. No way were they going to be put off what they came out to do in the first place, which was of course looting. They found three candles, five blankets, a *Rupert* book, knives, forks and spoons and even a tin opener, but the most surprising was a tin of spam that Trevor had found: S.P.A.M, Specially, Prepared, American, Meat.

"I have found our tea, Dave, we will go to Brown's greengrocery, go around the back and get some apples and carrots. I hid them on Saturday when I was working for them in the back yard, but I couldn't get them out. Mr Brown worked in the back all afternoon. "Did you hide anything, Trev, when you were working Saturday?" asked David.

"No," Trevor replied. "Mr Cartwright the manager was talking to Mrs Dovey who works there. I heard her saying 'Watch that Trevor, don't trust him, I have noticed certain items missing, Mr Cartwright,' so I didn't have the chance to get anything."

They went off to their den where they started to set up their home. Over a period of weeks they really got lots of items to fill their den. For two young boys they worked wonders. Whilst they were eating the spam and apple in the den they heard their sister Doreen shouting them. She did not know about their den, but she knew they were somewhere on the tip because she had overheard them talking about it.

Trevor said, "Come on, Dave, if we go around the back of the tip and come up from the other side she won't know where our den is."

"What do you want?" David shouted as he approached her form the rear. She almost jumped out of her skin.

"You horrible person, I hate you," she said, as she got hold of his arm whilst slapping the back of his head. "Nan wants to see you, she is really angry with you for not mopping the wash house floor."

"That was ages ago, we have seen her since then," said David. David said to Trevor, "Leave the talking to me; I can lie better than you."

"Thought we wasn't going back," Trevor said.

At that moment Doreen started to drag David by the arm, "You are coming home, Nan said I'm to bring you back, and take you back is what I'm going to do."

As they walked into the kitchen, Nan got David and shook him violently whilst slapping his head. "Where have you been, you horrible little boy?"

"Nan, Nan," David was shouting, "I was only thinking of you!"

"Stop it, Nan, we were doing it for you!" Trevor shouted with an angry expression.

"Did what for me?" Nan asked.

"That's what I have been trying to tell you," said David. We knew you hadn't got a pillow, so we went out to find you one."

"Well where is it then? And that was days ago, why haven't you been sleeping in the wash house?"

"We haven't found you one yet but I found this," he said, as he produced a brooch from his pocket.

"What a good boy you are, thinking of your nan," she said as she snatched it from his hand and held it up to the light.

David muttered under his breath, "I hate you, you old bag."

Just as he thought he had got away with lying to his nan, she got hold of his and Trevor's arms. "Right you can scrub the wash house from top to bottom," Nan ordered.

With a smirk their sister Doreen gave them a bucket and a scrubbing brush.

"So your mother did have a scrubbing brush after all, you little pair of liars," Nan angrily said. "Doreen you watch them and make sure they don't run off again."

Their Mom was upstairs and heard every word. She ran down the stairs – she was very angry with their nan. "How dare you treat them like that! Ninety percent of the food you eat they have got for us. I don't want you shouting at them anymore. If you want the wash house cleaned, then you scrub it."

"How dare you talk to me like that – I'm your mother."

"Yes, mother, and this is my house, not yours, these boys have suffered enough."

Doreen came running in. "Nan, they have run off again."

"Let them," replied Nan "I wash my hands of them. Let them run wild, your mother doesn't care, so why should I?"

That evening the boys spent the night in the den again but the weather proved to be too cold throughout the night – the wash house with Nan looked a better proposition.

The next morning they very sheepishly walked into the kitchen and their mother threw her arms around them. "Oh I've been so worried."

"We're ok, Mom. Where is Nan?"

"She has gone to stay at your aunt's house in Birmingham."

Both brothers at the same time said, "Oh good."

"You two are filthy; go and get cleaned up."

After a good wash down and some food they went off to see what they could find – to them it was finding, to the authorities it was looting. They went further than looting, it became breaking and entering; they were now fully pledged thieves. They had now entered a different lifestyle. After, they had burgled houses always when there was an air raid going on, this never bothered them. All the items they had stolen were buried inside their den. They dug a very big hole and lined it with

A VERY KIND LADY LIVES IN THIS COTTAGE

lino, and over the hole they placed old doors and boards from the tip. They had looted lots of jewellery, china and many toy trains. David thought when the war was over he could sell all the ill-gotten gains – he and Trevor could start their own business.

One day, as they were going through the rubble, they came upon a mother and her baby. Trevor went white and was violently sick.

David ran for the air-raid warden. "Please, mister, there is a body under the rubble, with a baby."

"A what?" said the warden. "What are you doing moving the rubble? I remember you," he said. "Where is your mate, he kicked me, didn't he?"

"No," David said very quietly. "The lady, mister, come quick." So they hurried to the spot where he and Trevor had been rummaging.

"There, mister, look, she might be alright," David explained.

"No, son," the warden replied, "she's a goner."

Trevor looked as white as a sheet; he even had a tear in his eye.

"How did you see the lady, were you up to no good?"

David had to think fast. "No mister, I saw the lady's hand sticking out from the rubble."

"Ok now you two clear off and don't let me see you two again. I know it was you that kicked me," he said pointing at Trevor.

"No, honest mister, it wasn't me."

Just at that moment another warden shouted, "Bert I need you here quick, I've just heard tapping coming from this house." He was pointing to a bombed house where he stood.

Trevor and David had run away from the warden whilst he was listening to his mate. "Dave," Trevor said, "I've ripped my trousers and I must get some better clothes."

"Ok," Dave said, "we will go to the edge of the city and see if there are any on the clothes lines; it's no good looking around here – nobody has got anything, besides, we know them all, we daren't take any of their clothes."

Trevor said, "They are no better than the clothes we are wearing, now let's go, it's a good walk to the edge of the city, it will be nice to see all the fields, trees and the animals."

It took then two and a quarter hours to reach the countryside; cottage after cottage – nothing.

"I'm getting hungry," David said.

"Me too," replied Trevor, "I'm going to knock on the door of the next cottage."

"What for Dave?" Trevor asked.

"To ask for a piece of bread," He replied.

"We will get a thick ear."

"We might not though, I'm hungry, Trev," Dave said "Let me do the talking."

An elderly lady opened the door. She had a little cap on with little blue flowers all over it and a pinny that matched her cap; she was a very red-faced lady and she had a very sweet smile. "Can I help you boys?"

"Please, lady, we are hungry and we haven't anywhere to stay, our house was bombed and we were lucky to get out."

"Where is your mommy?" the elderly lady asked.

"Killed in the bombing."

"You poor little devils! Come in and sit down, I've got stew – do you like stew?"

"Yes please," they both answered.

"There you are, and a piece of bread to go with it. I will get you a glass of milk," she said as she disappeared into the kitchen.

Dave said, "A, we picked the right house here."

After they had eaten, the old lady said, "Boys I've filled the tin bath for you, I have some clothes that belonged to my son when he was your age."

After they had washed up and looked nice and clean, the old lady put out two shirts, two jumpers and two pairs of trousers for them. The boys were full with food, had a new outfit and were very happy so they didn't need to steal that day – they had never known such kindness.

"Is there anything we can do for you?" the boys questioned.

"Yes, would you chop some wood for me, saw up some of those branches also will you, and fill the coal scuttle for me and light up the fire?"

When they had finished all the chores the old lady gave them a sandwich to take away with them. As they left they waved. "What a wonderful lady, Trev," Dave said. "I'm going to get a present for that lady."

"Good idea," Trev agreed. "We've been well fed, and look at these clothes – we don't half look posh and we didn't have to steal any of them."

The old lady had wrapped up their clothes for them to take away with them. David swung the bundle around his head twice and threw it over the hedgerow into the field.

As they walked, Trevor heard a train. "Dave, let's take the train home," Trevor suggested.

"Don't be daft, Trev, we haven't any money," replied David.

"Since when did we pay?"

"That's true," David said. "Ok, let's do it."

They waited over an hour for a train to come by, and when it finally came it was packed with mostly soldiers. "A Trev, we don't look scruffy do we? We can say our mother has our tickets."

"Oh yes, we can," replied Trevor. So on the train they got standing room only; being small they nudged their way into a space between the suitcases, with the swaying and the rocking of the coach they both fell fast asleep. Suddenly, as the cases were picked up they fell sidewards because they were leaning against the cases, and they were fully woken up by a cry of "All change!" from the porter, telling the passengers it was the end of the line.

"Trev, where are we?" asked David.

"Dunno," Trevor answered.

As they stepped off the train they asked a soldier "Where are we, mister?"

The soldier answered, "London, son."

"We have missed our stop Trev."

"Never mind, we have never been to London before."

"But it's getting dark," remarked David.

"That's ok, we can stay here for a while and look around, we can always get the train back."

They asked the ticket collector what time the last train back was, and he answered, "No more tonight, son, where is your ticket?"

"Our mom has them."

"Then why isn't she with you?"

"We lost her in the crowd; she should be here in a minute," they said as they pretended to look for her in the crowd.

"There she is. Mom, Mom we are here!"

As the ticket collector looked to see who they were waving to, they both ran passed him as fast as they could. "I'll get you next time," the ticket collector shouted.

Trevor said, "He won't, they never do; they always say that."

Whilst they were walking through the streets they were amazed at how different everywhere looked from the town they lived in. As they were looking for something to steal the air raid sirens were sounded, and a few minutes later bombs started to fall. They ran like headless chickens without knowing where they were running. A bomb fell on a street behind them – it sent a shock wave through the street where they were – it knocked them off their feet. They were covered in dust, coughing and choking. They both thought they had breathed their last breath. The fires were intense, and as the dust cleared they noticed lots of white sheets of paper scattered all over the place.

Trev said, "Dave, they are white five pound notes!" As quick as a flash they started to stuff them down their shirts, but suddenly they heard, "Come here you two, stand still" said an angry looking policeman.

"Come on, Trev, it's time to go!" shouted David. So once again they were running for what they thought were their lives, in and out the bombed buildings.

"This copper isn't gonna give up, Trev, he just keeps running."

Finally they lost the police officer as they hid themselves in a cellar of a bombed house.

"I'm going back to the station, Dave, we don't belong around here," remarked Trevor. So to the station they walked.

"This station looks different, Dave."

I WONDER WHERE THIS TRAIN GOES TO TREV

RUN DAVE THAT BOMB WAS CLOSE

"I know, it's not the one we came to earlier, look those wagons have covers over them."

So they crept towards the wagons and got inside one of them. There were empty wooden boxes inside the wagon they had climbed into so they got inside one of them; it was full of straw and felt warm and cosy. They soon fell asleep – they were there all night.

Next morning they got back onto the train home; it was packed again with soldiers. They used the same excuse that they had used on the way down to London. They asked a soldier where the train was heading. "To Birmingham, son."

"Great," Dave said excitedly, "we are heading in the right direction."

Trevor started to get the money out of his shirt, but David went barmy at him. "Stop that you idiot, wait until we get home."

When they finally got home they went straight into the wash house, locked the door and emptied their shirts of money. They had one hundred and ninety five pounds – they were rich.

"Right Trev, we will give Mom fifty and hide the rest."

"Good idea, Dave, where shall we hide it?"

"I know, let's get a brick out of the wall behind the copper." With an old rusty nail they scrapped the mortar from around the brick; it took a couple of hours to get it out. When they placed the money in the hole they found the brick would not go back so they took it in turns to chip away at the brick till finally the piece of house brick they were left with just fitted back in the hole. They filled the sides with mud so it wasn't noticeable and it looked ok. "No one ever goes behind the copper," said David.

They were too young to spend white five pound notes, so they decided to leave them where they were until the war was over.

"Let's give Mom this fifty pounds."

"Mom, we're home," they shouted as they walked in.

"Where have you been?" their mom asked.

"London," they replied.

"London? London?" she said in a loud voice. "How the hell did you afford to go there?"

WOW TREV A WALLET WITH MONEY IN IT WE ARE RICH.

"We didn't pay, we were coming home and we fell asleep on the train. You should have seen all the soldiers, Mom, there were thousands of them. Look what me and Trevor got you."

"Oh my God, my God, where did you get all this money? I've never held this much in my life!"

"We found it, Mom, in London; it was just lying on the ground so we picked it up for you."

"You two are good boys to your mother; I will take you to the pictures tonight."

"Great, what's on, Mom?" they said together.

"I don't know. It'll be good to go out without worrying about money. I will buy you some sweets as well, I've got plenty of coupons because I haven't bought sweets for a long time because I haven't had any money."

The boys were so exited.

"By the way, where did you get those nice clothes?"

"A lady gave them to us, and a lovely dish of stew with big chunks of meat, she's a wonderful lady, Mom, ever so kind," Trevor said.

"We did some chores for her and she said we could visit her any time. We are going to take her a present," said David.

"That's a lovely thought," Mom replied, "I'm sure that will make her happy to know someone cares."

So out they went to the wash house. Mother watched them as they disappeared into the building, and a thought came to her: that kind lady was the first person to show kindness to her boys. She saw how much that lady impressed them, and at that moment in time she felt at peace and a calm feeling came over her.

On the way to the cinema the boys never stopped talking.

"Look boys, it's George Formby on at the cinema."

"Who's George Formby? We were hoping it was going to be cowboys."

"Never mind boys, I'm sure you will enjoy it."

The interior looked incredibly posh to the boys and their mom. "Boys we'll go upstairs, we can really live it up tonight thanks to my two wonderful boys." She felt so proud as she hugged them both. Oh yes, now they were really excited.

Half way through the film an announcement came onto the screen: 'Air-raid imminent, those who wish to evacuate to the air-raid shelter please leave now.'

"What's that say, Mom?" asked David.

"Air-raid imminent. I'm not moving, I'm enjoying the film," said Mom.

"Good," the boys said, "we will stay as well." On the way home David said, "I really liked that George Formby; he's very funny and I like his singing."

"Not me," Trevor said. "The film was ok but I didn't like the singing."

"I really enjoyed it, boys, thanks to you. Are you boys working tomorrow?"

"Yes," they both answered at the same time.

"I will get you some potatoes, Mom," David said.

"I can't get anything at the moment, I'm being watched," Trevor told her, "but I will buy some meat out of my wages for you."

Back home the boys lit the fire under the copper. The bed chair that they had got for their nan was very comfortable and both David and Trevor were very fair with each other, they shared the bed equally – Trevor would have it one night, then David the next.

"What are we going to give that lady, Trev?"

"Remember that vase with all the flowers on it? I thought we could give her that."

"I was thinking of that brush and comb set we have from that big house we robbed, remember? I think it's real silver, Trev."

"I don't agree, Dave. Tell you what, if you spin that pop bottle, which one of us the cap points to will be the winner and that'll be the present we give to that nice lady."

"What if it stops half way?" Trevor said.

"Well whoever it's nearest to."

David spun the bottle and it stopped nearer to Trevor, so they took the vase to the old lady. She was overjoyed with the gift, and they did the same chores that they did the first time they where there.

She said, "Boy s, I have some eggs and bacon from the farmer, would you like some?"

It had been a long time since they had seen eggs or bacon, bacon was a really rare sight. "Oh yes please."

"And a thick slice of crusty bread, boys."

"You are a really kind lady," remarked Trevor.

"Yes, you are," agreed David.

They ate it so quickly, and not a crumb was left. "Thank you very much, lady."

"Come any time, boys. Have an egg each but take care not to break them."

"Oh thank you, you are so kind."

She loved the happy look on their little faces; little faces indeed, they were much older in their minds than their exterior showed.

When they finally reached home they both shouted, "Mom, we've got two eggs for you."

"You haven't stolen them, have you?"

"No, Mom, honest; that old lady gave them to us, and we thought you could have them boiled – we know you like boiled eggs."

"Yes, I do, thank you boys. What would your mom do without you? You are good boys." She told them that on a daily basis; she always praised them up – she loved them so much.

That night they went out stealing from a house they found was very easy to rob when there was an air-raid. The houses they robbed were either middle class or posh houses as they called them. They lived this lifestyle right up to the end of the war.

One day their mother said, "Boys the war is over, it's back to school next week." This was a massive shock to them, they had been free for so long.

When back at school they became very unruly, and they were caned by the headmaster nearly every week. They kept playing truant. They were both caught rummaging through the rubble of a bombed house when they should have been at school. Two police officers caught hold of them and Trevor started shouting and kicking the policeman, so the officer hit him so hard he didn't know what day it was. When they were in the police station their mother came in and Trevor ran to her and gave her a great big hug – he was thinking if the policeman saw him do that the he would be a little sympathetic towards him. Mother said, "Boys, I can't help you this time."

The boys were kept overnight in the police cells and they appeared before the judge the next morning. "You have become very unruly," the judge announced. "I am sending you both to a correction facility where you will learn to be better citizens. I am sentencing you to three to six years, and I hope when you are released you will have become worthy of living with society and will have learned some skills to help you in life. Take them away," the judge ordered.

They felt so bad as they were led away because they could see and hear their mother sobbing really loudly.

All the time they were incarcerated Trevor was taught a lot about electrics and David was taught carpentry and building skills. They spent five years in the correction facility altogether and when they finally came out their mother was waiting outside, it became a very tearful reunion.

"Come on boys, I have done you a very special lunch," Mom told them.

When they reached home all the neighbours were waving flags and shouting "welcome home" and tables were laid out just like the time when they celebrated the end of war. David had tears running down his cheeks; Trevor held them back, but they had a good time.

They were now young men, and for the first time David noticed feelings that he had never felt before, because there, giving him looks that were the looks of a young woman, was the girl he had grown up with, and she was now a beautiful woman. All his nerves were telling him just that. She walked right up to him and hugged and kissed him like he had never been kissed before. His heart was pounding.

"Would you allow me to be your woman?"

"Woman?" he said.

“Girlfriend,” she smiled. “I’ve always loved you but you never knew I was around, did you?”

His manhood was most certainly showing; he knew he wanted her and for the first time he experienced love just by looking at her.

When the boys finally got to bed they laughed very loudly for they were back in the wash house but they both had a proper mattress.

“Trev, I’m in love,” David said in a trembling voice.

“Who with?” Trev asked.

“June, the girl two doors away.”

“Oh yes, I saw you kissing her; she is a beauty now, Dave. I wonder if our goods are still in the den.” Trevor wasn’t really interested in David’s love life.

“I doubt it, Trev, we will have a look tomorrow. I really am in love, Trev.”

“I know, Dave, I can tell by your voice. Ask her out tomorrow.”

“Yeah I will. Hey I forgot, blimey Trev, is our money still behind that brick?”

With a quick look he said, “Yes, it’s still there Dave, it looks the same. It’s never been cleaned behind here – we were right to pick this as our hidey hole.”

“Trev, I’ve been thinking, we could open our own junk shop if our goods are still down that hole.”

“That’s a great idea, Dave. However we don’t know the first thing about selling.”

“I know that, Trev, I’m going to the library to get books and learn about antiques and selling; I’m sure some of the items might be old and worth a bit.”

“I’ll go to the council tomorrow to see about a shop and the rent they will want,” said Trevor.

The council were only too happy to rent them a shop when they were ready to rent.

The next morning they went to the tip, and to their surprise there was their den and it hadn’t even been touched, but there had been other children using it as their den. They never knew that underneath their feet were a lot of stolen items. When the boys looked inside the den

QUICK TREV I THOUGHT I HEARD SOMEONE COMING.

they could see the floor had not been touched. When the children had left the den that same evening, Dave and Trevor took up the floor and there before them were all of their ill gotten gains, so they very carefully replaced the floor of the den so no one would see it had been disturbed.

"Right, let's go to the council to get that shop."

The shop they were given was eight pounds a week and double fronted – it was used as a drapery shop before the war. All the counters and glass cabinets were still in situ.

"This is perfect! Right, we will get some sacks, Trev and tomorrow we will get all of our goods from the den."

The next evening as they uncovered the goods, Trevor remarked.

"We got a real good selection here, Dave."

"I know, Trev, but we need more."

"More, Dave? Are we breaking and entering tonight, then?"

"Yes, we are; are you losing your nerve, Trev?" David asked.

"No!" he shouted. "I was hoping we could start with what we had for the shop and put robbery behind us. If we are caught again we could face a seven year sentence, Dave."

"Well, let's see how it goes tonight."

It went well – jewellery, toys, even furniture; they worked all through the night.

Next morning their mom and sister Doreen turned up to help. They scrubbed, polished, and cleaned the windows – it looked just like one of those posh high street shops. Trevor and David came in through the back door with a sack of goods in each hand.

"What have you there, boys? Mom asked.

"Goods for the shop, Mom, we have been out buying."

"Wow." Doreen gasped when she saw all the beautiful jewellery.

"We have lots more as well," Dave said, smiling.

"Ok, son, you go and fetch it and we will display it all," Mom suggested.

It took nearly all day. When it was finished it looked so much like a china shop – plates, vases, statues on one side and a jewellery shop on the other side.

The next day after they had opened at 9am, Mother, sister Doreen and little sister Janet came to help, and to David's surprise Mom had even brought June to help sell the goods in the shop. Every time David looked at her he went weak at the knees.

"I've brought June; she would like a job working with you," Mom explained.

"Yes, yes, what a brilliant idea, but I haven't taken any money yet so how can I pay you if we don't sell anything?"

"I will work for free until it works," June answered.

"Dave, we have that money behind the brick in the wash house," Trevor told David.

"Of course we have. Tell you what, June, there are three bedrooms and a bathroom upstairs and a living room at the back of the shop, if I buy a bed for each room, Trev has one, I will have one and you could have on – you could live here rent free. Would your dad allow that?"

"I will ask him tonight."

"Bring him and your mom and show them that you will have your own room – it's got a lock and a key."

"I'm so excited," June said to David's mom.

"You love my son, don't you?"

"Oh yes very much, I always have, as far back as I can remember," she answered.

"Well you two make a lovely couple," Mom replied.

"I want to marry him and have his children, but please don't tell him, will you?"

"I won't," Mother assured her.

Trevor said, "Dave, could I have a word, would you mind if I don't live in the shop?"

"Why, Trev?" David asked.

"Look she loves you; a blind person could see that. I would be in the way and I know you would like to be alone with her."

"Thanks Trev. Look we will split that money fifty-fifty tonight, ok?"

"That's fine, Dave," Trevor agreed.

So that is what they did. They named the shop D&T Goods, and they both had their names on the rent book. Five o'clock came, so they closed the doors and started counting their takings; altogether there were twenty-seven pounds and ten shillings – they were all very happy.

The next morning, the two lads went to the bank to open an account; mother was so proud of them both.

The three bedrooms were fully furnished and June moved in after the first week. The living room was furnished as well. June was so happy and they all had a key, but there was rule that no one would come back to the shop after hours unless it was agreed – this was only for June for her privacy – if anyone did need to come back they would ring the bell. David and Trevor left the ladies to run the shop whilst they went out to find new stock; some was bought and some stolen.

Two and a half months passed, and all was going well – everyone was making money and life was looking very good for the future. After the shop was shut that evening the time came to retire to bed. They kissed goodnight, and June said, "Dave, thank you so much for all that you have done for me."

"You are welcome, June." He kissed her cheek and went to bed.

Just as he was dropping off to sleep he felt a silky, soft, warm body embrace him – June couldn't wait for him any longer.

The very next day they were engaged and she picked the ring from the shop stock. As mother and Doreen walked in for work, Mother looked at June, smiled, put her arms around her and hugged her tight. "You are a woman now June, aren't you?"

"Yes," she replied as she was going very red.

"He will look after you."

"We got engaged this morning," June told her happily.

"I am glad, June. He took his time, didn't he?"

"Oh Mother," June laughed. "You don't mind me calling you Mother do you?"

"I quite like it actually," Mother responded.

"I love him so I am going to work hard for him; I will make him so happy he will be in heaven for the rest of his life – I will make sure of that" June said.

"He is a lucky man," remarked David's mom.

"I'm the lucky one, Mother," replied June.

Just then David came into the shop, and his mom threw her arms around him. "Congratulations, son, you made a wise choice."

"Do you really think so, Mom?" David said.

"Oh yes, she will make you very happy – look at her dusting and polishing; she wants everything perfect for you."

"I will look after her. I haven't told her yet but I'm going to take her around town this afternoon and buy her lots of beautiful clothes. Could you mind the shop, Mom?"

"Of course I will, son."

"Thanks Mom."

"There is so much happiness I think I'm going to cry," she said emotionally, as she mopped up a tear from her cheek. "I do hope it will always be like this."

A couple of days later, at two in the afternoon, David said, "Mom have you seen Trevor?"

"No," she replied, "not for a couple of days."

"Me neither," he said.

About an hour or so after, Trevor walked in with a beautiful looking girl on his arm. "Folks, I would like all of you to meet Betty, my girlfriend."

After all the hugging and kissing was over, Trevor said, "Dave could I have a word in private?"

"Yes, what's wrong?" David asked.

"Nothing," Trevor replied. "Betty has nowhere to live – her granddad died last week and she is being turned out of her house. Her parents were killed in the bombing. I can't ask her to sleep in the wash house, Dave, can you help me please?"

"Trev this is half your shop, and there is a spare bedroom here that is yours as you know. Has she got a job?"

"No, she was looking after her granddad." Trevor explained.

"Ok, would she work with June? By the way, we got engaged a couple of days ago."

"That's great, Dave, June is a lovely girl."

"Yeah, I love her to bits," Dave said happily. "Listen I want all the gossip of how and where you two met. If you think she would get engaged to you, why don't you ask her to pick a ring from our shop stock?" David suggested.

"Oh yes, what a brilliant idea!" Trevor agreed.

These two brothers were as close as two brothers could be. They looked after each other and would die for each other, but they weren't brothers at all, which they didn't even know.

Trevor went into the shop and asked Betty if she would one day marry him, and with a very loud scream she jumped on him and kissed him repeatedly, like a chicken pecking corn.

"Oh yes, yes, yes," she screamed, everyone was so happy, "what a wonderful week this has been," mother was saying, as she mopped yet another tear from her cheek. Trevor told Betty, "pick a ring, any one you want and then we will be engaged to be married, I am so happy," he said with a smile on his face.

Betty ran to June and put her arms around her with floods of tears running down her face, saying, "You are such a wonderful family, oh June, I'm so happy."

June was in tears, Mother was in tears, even David was, but Trevor fought hard and was holding his back. "Right, close the shop, June, we're going to celebrate."

That evening they all went to the best restaurant they knew. Mother stood up with a glass of wine in her hand. "God Bless this family, and congratulations to you all and may happiness be yours always."

David stood up with his glass of wine and added, "I promise never to let any of my family down; I will protect and look after them until my last breath is taken, and I welcome June and Betty into our family."

Then Trevor stood up. "All he just said, I agree with and will do likewise, and a big thank you to our wonderful mother." There were tears all around, but what they had not noticed was all the customers were cheering and clapping and all the ladies were wiping their eyes, it was a romantic evening.

The morning after, all four of them, Trevor, Betty, David and June sat around the table having breakfast; the atmosphere was as good as life could be. After the girls had washed all the dishes, David said, "Don't open the shop yet please, I've something to say. Me and June like running this shop and living here ourselves as a couple – don't look worried, Betty, we are all family now and we will look after each other as I promised last night, but I've been thinking, Trev, I woke early this morning and my mind was full of all sorts of ideas. What I thought, Trev, and I hope you agree, the shop next door is empty; we could rent that as well as this shop, and as we have lots of jewellery, I was thinking you and Betty could run that as a jewellers. We could furnish it as we have this shop and decorate it from top to bottom so you and Betty can have a home the same as me and June have here."

Before he could say another word, both girls ran to him and kissed him with such love. Betty then ran to Trevor and said; "It was the luckiest day of my life when I met you and your family. That's a great idea, Dave, what shall we call it, the same as this?"

"Yes, D&T, instead of goods just jewellers, we will still be equal partners in both shops," David said.

"You are so kind, David, would you allow me and June to pick all the curtains and furniture for our home?" Betty asked in a sweet quiet voice.

"Of course. Trev will give you the money you need to buy whatever. We can close up early and see the council about signing up for the shop – they are expecting us, hope you don't mind Trev I thought about the shop next door and made enquiries, but I wasn't sure so I made the appointment in case. When you came in with Betty you broke my dream. I did ask if we took on both shops would they consider a rent reduction and I was told yes," David explained.

"Great Dave, let's do it!"

So all was put into place, with all the items coming into the shop that people wished to sell.

"Trev, I don't think we will need to steal anymore."

"Hope not, Dave, things are looking up."

After two weeks the jewellery shop was opened. Betty soon picked up the whys and wherefores of the business. People were buying and

D&T Jewellery.
OPEN

selling, and Trevor got to know a high street jeweller who was buying all the expensive jewellery that came into the shop. Trevor always took whatever money that was made from selling the better pieces and split it fifty-fifty; this money was never put through the books. They all went from strength to strength. David and June were selling toys now and stocking new toys from the manufacturer – Hornby trains and even some foreign toys. Trevor and Betty were excelling with the jewellery shop.

One day Trevor thought long and hard and said, "Dave, we could buy a big store or an arcade."

"That's worth thinking about, Trev, ok let's look into it."

"Dave, what I thought was an arcade with lights, coloured lights displaying our name at each end."

"That's a brilliant idea, Trev, oh yes I like that, we could make a long store with just us in the arcade; we could rent the shops out. What do you think? Let's go and see the council tomorrow, I've got twenty-six thousand pounds underneath the floorboards, Trev."

"So have I, Dave," replied Trevor.

"Ok look we need to cook the books so we can put this money through the business, well most of it anyway."

"Tell you what, Dave, I'm going to order a van with our shop name on it, then everyone will get to know who and where we are."

"Tell you what, Trev, I will go to the council tomorrow, you go and order two vans, one each, and I will leave you to do the designs on the sides."

"Now we are motoring," said Trevor.

When they told the girls of their plans they were very excited.

"June, when we get all what we plan into action, will you marry me?"

"Yes please, oh yes please!"

Betty hugged them both. "I have something to tell you, I have booked a table at our favourite restaurant, hope that's ok"

"Yes, that's fine," they both replied.

So at the restaurant Dave, June and Betty were waiting for Trevor to turn up. Twenty minutes later in walked Trevor. "Sorry I'm late I have been doing a deal with the jeweller – I'll tell you about it tomorrow Dave."

"Ok, Trevor," replied Dave.

The waiter came over with a bottle of champagne. "Hello," they all said together. When all the glasses were filled, Betty stood up raised her glass and wished David and June a very happy life together and congratulated them on their decision to get married.

Trevor jumped from his chair, "Married! that's great," he said as he shook David's hand and kissed June. "Congratulations; I'm very happy for you both."

"I have something else to say," announced Betty. "I hope this doesn't spoil the celebrations."

Trevor looked at Betty very worriedly, "What is it, Betty, come on, tell."

"Well I've been putting this off for some time because of all the plans you have been working on."

"Come on, Betty, what is it?"

She turned and looked at Trevor. "Darling, you are going to be a daddy."

Trevor's mouth opened, his eyes grew wide, he dropped his glass of champagne which smashed on the floor, his arms went up and he shouted at the top of his voice, "I'M GOING TO BE A DADDY!"

The whole of the restaurant cheered and clapped. As David and Trevor were now well known to everyone in the restaurant they all came over and kissed Betty and shook Trevor's hand. June and Dave were delighted.

"I was so afraid to tell you because of all the plans you were making."

Dave said, "We could have a double wedding – that would be marvellous. What do you think, Betty?"

"Well he hasn't asked me yet."

So on one knee Trevor went, "My adorable Betty, will you marry me?"

With tears cascading down her face, she threw her arms around him, "Yes, yes, yes, oh, yes!"

"I'm so happy, Trevor," said Dave.

"We will rename the shop D&T Family Shop."

"Ok, that's fine with me," agreed David.

Next day David purchased from the council Southern Arcade. "Would you mind if I called it The Family Arcade, with our name above it?" David asked.

"That's fine," answered the man as he signed the deeds and made the change of name on the documents.

All done, now to clean up the arcade, I want this arcade to be the most posh and the best arcade in England, David thought to himself.

Back at the shop he told the good news to the ladies. They screamed, "It's so exciting being with you two brothers, with something always going on!"

Trevor walked in. After hearing what David had done he was as excited as everyone. "Now we will show them what two little urchins can achieve. I've ordered the vans, Dave, and here is the design I came up with."

"Wow! You have done us proud, Trev."

"Well ditto to that, Dave, are we a team or are we a team? Right let's ask Mom and sister to look after the shop for a couple of hours whilst we go and look over the arcade, and we can say what and how we want everything. Yes, you ladies can say what you would like to have and the colour scheme you think would look best. On the outside," Trevor added, "I would like dark green with gold lines and lettering, I've seen that in a picture somewhere and I liked it."

"Sounds good to me, what do you think ladies?" David asked.

"Yes," they both replied, "sounds nice."

"With brass lamps over the windows lighting up the goods inside the shop window," David added.

"That sounds absolutely wonderful," Betty said, "What do you think, Jane?"

"Yes, yes, also I would like to see gold leaf put on that iron work at both ends of the arcade."

"That sounds good. With the brass lamps, dark green paintwork, gold lettering and thin gold lines all around the eight shops and then

D&T
GOODS.
D&T
JEWELLERY.

gold leaf on the iron work at both ends, our name in lights at both ends of the arcade lit up at night, boy it will look great." Trevor said.

"Right, let's go around all the firms that do all this type of work and get it open as soon as possible," David suggested.

"Yes let's do it," they all agreed.

"Before we go, I was thinking, shall we rent the four shops on the one side then keep the other four ourselves? That way the rent we would get could pay for all our overheads for our four shops and the arcade would still be ours?"

"I like that idea, Dave. What do you ladies say?"

"Yes, it will mean we can retail for little or no expense to us."

"Ok, we will do it; I will put an ad in the evening paper for tomorrow."

They started contacting all the builders, electricians and the people that did the gold leaf work. On his way home David thought, I will pop in and talk to my solicitors.

"Have you thought of building your own store to your own dimensions?" asked the solicitor.

"I couldn't afford that at the moment," David answered.

"Yes you can with your track record, now the bank would back you"

"Really?" David said, shocked.

"Oh yes no problem."

"I will go and discuss that with my brother this evening. Where would I be able to build such a store?"

"Almost anywhere, there is a lot of demolition going on at this moment in time. I have a map of all the areas that are going to be demolished and the council are asking for architects to send plans in with drawings of the type of buildings that would make the areas better."

When David received the plans to David's horror he saw that his mother's house was going to be one of those to be pulled down. "Right I want you to purchase that block of houses and the land surrounding it," David ordered.

"Why?" asked the solicitor.

ARCADE

"Because that's my mom's house and that wash house was where I lived most of my young life; there were ten of us in our family – me and my brother lived in that wash house."

"Well I don't... I can't... I mean... you actually lived in a wash house?"

"Yes we did. It holds many memories and I don't want to see it demolished."

"Ok I will start the ball rolling," said the solicitor.

"It is very important to me. I'm off to see the bank manager, see about financing the store."

"What exactly are you thinking of doing?"

"If I can purchase that block of houses to save them and then purchase these other blocks that are bombed and damaged, I could demolish all those, build my store there and incorporate my mom's block of houses for the grounds of the store and preserve them for, well, at least my lifetime. And two doors away from my mom's house is where my future wife lived," David told him.

"Oh I see, right, I will go all out to secure all the ground you require; in the meantime could you complete a little sketch of the building you wish to build?"

"Well, you know that Victorian red terracotta building in the high street, it's a gentleman's outfitters?" David asked the solicitor.

"Yes, I know the one."

"Well I want my building to look exactly like that."

"Oh right," replied the solicitor, "I will get the architect started right away on that design."

"I will let you have the interior layout tomorrow after I've talked it over with my partners."

David went to the bank and he was offered the amount he had asked for. He told the bank manager that if his brother Trevor agreed to it they would go for it. David went home to explain to Trevor what he had done.

"Great idea, Dave, let's go for it, they aren't knocking my mom's house down."

The ladies were not as sentimental as their men folk but they still went along with the idea. Whilst all that was going on, the arcade was up and running. It was a great success and dozens of people were in the store all day long. They kept the shops where they started from, mainly because David was very sentimental about things; he couldn't stand change, where as Trevor wasn't quite the same, he would have sold the shops. All was agreed, they purchased the block of houses that his mom and future wife had lived in.

That year they had their double wedding. They only had a small do, the ladies did not want to waste any money as the building of their store was costing a large amount of money.

When Betty gave birth to a nine pound boy they named him David. David was very proud, and he and June became David's Godparents. It turned out David and June could not have children, but they were so much in love they felt they had it all anyway. They would play a big part in David's life anyway as the years rolled by so really they had a son after all, even though he belonged to Trevor and Betty.

The store was finished – it was beautiful, with carpets everywhere, gold leaf iron work everywhere, brass lamps, lifts, moving stairs, a wonderful restaurant and even a doorman in a red uniform with gold braid on it. The store was featured in all magazines and newspapers, even on the Patha news in all the cinemas. Thousands of people came to the opening of the shop, and some just for the free food – well it was a grand affair.

June had been looking for David all over the store. Betty and Trevor couldn't find him either. Then Trevor said, "I know where he will be; you two go have a cup of tea in the restaurant, I will be back as soon as I find him."

Trevor went to the old wash house, and sure enough David was there just sitting down and staring. "Hi, mind if I join you Dave?" Trevor asked.

"No, not at all, come in and sit down. I've made some tea would you like a cup?"

"Yes please, is that the same tea pot and cups we used when we lived here?"

"Yes they are, I saved them when we opened our first shop so I got them out of the storage yesterday. I love it in here, Trev, I'm at home.

I remember my humble start in life when I sit here. They could knock down all of our shops and it would make me sad, Trev, but if they knocked Mom's house down and this wash house it would break my heart. Promise me, Trevor, that you will never allow anyone to pull this down while you or me are still living," David asked.

"You have my promise, Dave," Trevor reassured him.

"I want your son to inherit all what me and you have worked for."

"Thanks, Dave, you can rely on me. Listen Dave," Trevor said, "I've just had an idea. These houses are in the walled grounds of the store, aren't they?"

"Yes," David answered.

"Let's renovate them to their former glory, put everything back into it that they would have had when they were first built."

"The only one that still has its original fittings is Mom's house so we know exactly what we would need. All the gardens could be put back as they were with the same blue brick paths and the fences," David said.

At that point, Trevor laughed.

"What's funny?" asked David.

"The fences, we pinched all of them, remember, to give Mom, bless her, for her fire and for the fire under the copper."

David gave a muffled laugh, he was chocking on his tears when all the memories of his mother and childhood came back.

"It's ok, Dave," Trevor said as he put his arm around him, "Let's go round the houses and look, Dave, see what you think after going into the second house."

"Ok, Trev, let's go for it."

"Great," said Trevor. "What I thought was, we could open them to the public all through the summer at a small cost. We could have tables and chairs in each garden, only if they ordered tea though, otherwise we could put them in the far corner of the yard and not on the gardens as it would give people the feeling of days gone."

"I wouldn't want the wash house touched," David replied.

"No I know; it would just be done up to preserve the brick work. Not only that, Dave, we could also make Mom's house and the wash house the centre attraction – this would show people who we are, where we came from, how we lived and what we have achieved."

"That's a good idea, Trev, let's go and tell the girls our plans."

"Hey, Dave, I've just thought, we could get them listed and then nobody would ever be allowed to touch them."

"Good idea, Trev, as soon as they are finished I will go and see the council and get that done."

The girls were over the moon with the idea; June was so happy to know her mom's house would be put back to its original condition.

Dave and Trevor looked in every scrap yard to find the original fireplaces. They thought if they found them they would know they were the right ones and in good condition; they even went round all the reclaimed timber yards to find the original doors and the floor quarry tiles. They found all the original items, and all was delivered to David's and Trevor's terraced houses. They even bought a very big shed – this was erected to keep all the doors, fire gates, tiles and even the picture rails, so nothing could be broken or indeed stolen. They found everything they needed, so the builders moved in. David was very protective of his wash house – no one was allowed near it; he had a barrier placed all around it. The wash house was his pride and joy. The one thing they both agreed on was brand new slate for the roofs – they also agreed that lead flashing would be used around the chimney.

Then came the day when they were all finished. They looked better than the day they had been built. All the gardens were finished as they would have been – low fences, blue brick path and a little fence and a gate to each garden; even the paint was original, they had purchased it from the council yard. When you lived in a council house you had the choice of three colours – brown, green or cream, and you could have any of these colours mixed up; for example you could have brown on the bottom and cream or green on the top or vice versa. David had all the houses done in different combinations of colours. The outside of the wash house was repainted; David would not allow the inside to be touched and it was laid out exactly the way the boys had lived in it. All the information was written on a board screwed to the wall with a photo of David and Trevor so people could see where these millionaires came from and what is possible in life.

David was sitting in the wash house with the door open looking at the houses. Trevor walking up the path said, "Look good, don't they?"

"Thanks, Trev, you have had some great ideas but this is your best one, I almost don't want people to walk around them."

"I know what you mean, Mom would have loved these," David said.

With a giggle, Trevor looked at David and said, "Now don't go pinching the palings for the fire while I'm gone." They both had a good laugh and then went back to the store.

To their surprise, the next day newspaper men and film crews were all there to take pictures and films of the restored houses – they were in every newspaper and shown in every cinema; they were a hit all over England, Wales, Scotland and Ireland. People came from everywhere to see how two backward boys had made it this far in life.

David now spent most of his time showing the people around the houses. He always felt proud when explaining how he and Trevor lived in the wash house. Trevor was more for the shops, they were his love. Trevor's son David would sit with his Uncle David in the wash house and drink tea from the same cup that his dad drank from when he was a boy, and he listened to the same stories a hundred times over; he became as much attached to that wash house as his Uncle David was.

One day, little David walked into the wash house and found his uncle writing in a book. "What are you writing, Uncle Dave?" he asked.

"I'm writing about mine and your dad's life," David answered.

"Isn't that called an autobiography?"

"Yes, something like that, it's a long book about three hundred pages."

"What are you going to call the book?"

"I've called it... I'm not sure yet I haven't thought of a title yet."

"Shall I think of a title for you?"

"No, its ok, David, it's mine to think of a title. Tell you what, would you like to go for a walk?"

"Where to?"

"To a place that me and your dad used to go to."

Ten minutes later they came to a grassed parkland. "This used to be a rubbish tip; me and your dad spent many hours here."

"What, on a tip full of rubbish?"

"Yes you would be amazed at the things people used to throw away. Anyway, see that big tree over there; we had a den behind that."

"People would see you, a den is supposed to be hidden."

"Well then, there were brambles covering it, we found a way into it."

"Let's have a closer look," said little David.

"Go on then," his uncle said. As they got closer to the tree little David and Uncle David could see a big hole that for some unknown reason had never been filled in.

"Corr, it's deep, isn't it?"

"Yes," he replied. "We had a lot of loo"

"A lot, Uncle, a lot of what?"

"I was thinking out loud, it was a lot to do for two young boys."

"What boys?"

"Me and your dad, we dug that hole out."

"How old were you?"

"I'm not sure; about 8 or 9."

"What did you dig it out with?"

"With an old coal shovel we found on the tip and an iron bar."

"That must have been hard work?"

"Yes, we worked all night."

"Uncle, look what I've found stuck in the side of the hole – it looks like a ring."

"Well I'll be blowed!"

"Can I keep it, Uncle?"

"Of course you can my dear boy, of course you can. Tell you what, that is a real diamond. You save it until you get a girlfriend and when you ask her to marry you, if she says yes, then you can put that ring on her finger; that means she is yours and you are hers and you are engaged to be married."

"You mean we own each other?"

"Sort of, yes."

"It's all so confusing, I don't think I will bother with girls."

David laughed. "You will, my boy, you will."

Little David pulled a face. "I hate girls, they are so soppy."

"Tell you what, fancy a drive in my car?"

"Yes, Uncle, that would be great!"

"Funny, your dad always says that."

"Says what?"

"Great, whenever he liked anything or did things he liked he always said great."

"Ha, ha, so I'm just like my dad then?"

"Oh yes, you are very much like your dad. Now go and tell your mom or dad I'm taking you for a drive in the country side."

"Ok, I will be back in a minute, Uncle Dave."

David got his Morris Minor out. It was his first car and he could not part with it. It was in wonderful condition as he had had it restored. "Uncle, are we going in this little old car? Why not the big car, I love that one much more?"

"This is a little Morris Minor, the big one is a Rolls Royce – it's not got a patch on this one," said his Uncle Dave.

"What's a patch?"

"That just means I prefer this one – I prefer to drive this one."

"I like the big one with its soft seats and lots of room."

"Who did you tell you were going out?"

"My mom," said David.

"That's ok then."

"Where are we going?"

"I'm going to show you a little cottage where a very kind lady put some faith back into two little boys that had no faith or trust."

"Faith, Uncle?"

"Yes, faith. You see, we thought as we were growing up nobody helped anybody like me and your dad. We were out of control and had to look after ourselves. When we came down here we walked, by the way, yes, walked all this way from where we just came. Yes we did... ah, there it is."

"What is?"

"That little cottage."

"It's not very big, Uncle, is it?"

"You have been spoilt, that's why you are saying that. We came down here to stea... to... to..." He nearly forgot himself; he nearly told him that he went down there to steal. "Anyway, we were hungry so I knocked on the door and I asked the lady if she had a piece of bread – we told her a little white lie."

"What was that, Uncle Dave?"

"I can't remember now. She called us in, gave us a bath and some really nice clothes that were her son's, and we sat down to a dish of stew and a piece of crusty bread. We did some chores for her, cut wood and filled the coal scuttle, and on our way out she gave us an egg each."

"Only one each, Uncle?"

"Ah, the war was still on – eggs were hard to get."

When they got back Betty was waiting for them. "Have you had a nice ride out with Uncle David?"

"Yes, Mom, he showed me where my dad and Uncle David had a dish of stew off an old lady."

"You do like to reminisce, David, don't you?"

"It's what keeps me going, Betty, I've no interest in money or business anymore. Sitting with my June looking at our old houses and remembering the past, that's what I love."

"Funny thing, that is David, Trevor is always going on about you pair and when you were boys. I hear the same stories all the time yet I never get tired of hearing them. I remember the very first time I walked into your shop with Trevor and he told me what a wonderful couple you and June were – I had only known him a couple of days, I was so scared. You put your arms around me and so did June; you were so loving and kind. You took me in when I had nothing, and you made me welcome." Tears were once again cascading down her face. "I've been so happy ever since that day; you are the kindest, most loving people, and I love you all so very much." She threw her arms around David's neck and sobbed her heart out.

David also had tears running down his face. "We love you very much Betty, you have made our Trevor a very happy man. You are the best sister-in-law."

Betty looked at David, and with tears still running down both of their faces, she said, "I've wanted to tell you that, David, from the very first day I got to meet you and June, but I've never found the courage until now."

"Oh, dear, sweet Betty, we have always known how grateful you are, but it's us that should be grateful to you for allowing us into your life."

Feeling like he wasn't sure how he felt, he went and sat in the wash house. For reasons he couldn't explain he always felt safe and at ease in there. He started on his book again. This is going to be a long job writing this book, he thought. Oh well, got nothing better to do these days.

June came through the door. "I've brought you a cup of tea; will it disturb you if I sit here with you?"

"Not at all, my darling, you are always welcome and wanted by my side."

"Thank you, you say the sweetest things – you always have; I've never known you to lose your temper or be cross, David."

"I've no need to, I love you all and we all get on so well, so how can I? You are all so sweet and good, I've never had any reason too... corr, I'm really starting to desire you..." As he was about to put his arm round her, the door flew open.

"Hello, am I interrupting anything?"

"No, not yet anyway," replied June with a smile.

"How is Betty? She was very tearful," asked David.

"I know, she loves our family so much because of what a wonderful reception we gave her when no one, not even I, really knew anything about her, and we have all looked after each other as a family and she is still grateful after all this time – she is a true family member," replied David.

Just then Betty walked down to the wash house with a tray, followed by little David. "I thought we could all have a cuppa and a scone and enjoy each other's company for a while." "That's a wonderful idea," June said.

"Thank you, Betty," Trevor said, as he put his arm around her and kissed her on the cheek.

"Uncle Dave, may I go and look around the houses please?" asked little David.

"I don't mind but it's up to your dad and mom."

"Can I, please? said little David as he looked at his mom. "Yes of course you can," his mom answered. "Be careful going up and down these stairs, they are quite steep."

"I know, Mom, I've been in the houses before."

"Well just be careful, and no running."

Trevor said, "You know why he asked you, Dave, if he could go in the houses?"

"Well, I did wonder really, seeing how you two are here."

"We always say to him you must never go in those houses without asking uncle Dave, they are his pride and joy," his dad told him, but they are as much yours as mine Trevor, "Dave I only did it for you, I love them, yes I do but I'm not passionate about them like you are," Trevor told him. "I went half in with you because we have never done anything on our own, and I like it that way, that will never change as far as I'm concerned, they are yours. Well when David is eighteen all my shares are being transferred to him." June was really happy about me doing that. "Is that ok with you two?" June threw her arms around David and said you are the best husband ever.

Once again Betty was in floods of tears, and for the first time Trevor could not hide his true feelings – he sobbed on June's shoulders and Betty once again on David's. "You really are the best, you two," said Trevor.

"Yes you are," Betty agreed.

"No, we are a family, we stick together, we are all the best together. Right, who is for tea and scones? I will be mother for a change," David said. "I do so love sitting here and looking at the gardens and houses. I can see me and June and all the children playing; it only seems like last week. I can always see our mom and June's mom sitting outside on the wooden chairs – they always appeared to be jolly, smiling and laughing. How they were able to cope with the hardships those two poor ladies suffered I will never know.

"Just shows how strong the will is in life," Betty replied. "Well, you and Trevor suffered and you came through it all – that's a credit to you both," she said as she kissed them both. She went to June, kissed her and said, "So did you."

"Well Betty, you did as well, losing your mom and dad in the bombing; living with your granddad then losing him and being told you had to leave your house. We all had our share, didn't we?"

"That's when I met Trevor. I was told I had to vacate the house in two days. I had no money, the furniture was worn out with age – no one wanted it. I went to the shop to get half a loaf but when I got there I found I was a penny short so they wouldn't let me have the bread, I was hungry. I felt so desperate and alone I started to cry, and Trevor came walking by and he stopped and asked if I was alright. I just broke down and sobbed for a good ten minutes before he could get any sense out of me. When I told him what was happening he told me 'it's alright I will help you'. I was really worried, I mean, I didn't even know him but I was so hungry. Granddad had been put in a pauper's grave, I was alone and afraid. I was lost, just lost. Trevor went into the shop and bought a bag of groceries, took me back home sat me down and did a meal for me. He told me not to worry and said 'I'm just going out for a little while but I will be back, I promise'. He went to see someone he knew to empty the house for me. The next day he paid the rent I owed, and cooked the dinner for me. Both nights he stayed on the settee just to make sure I was alright. He was and is a perfect gentleman; he spent two nights with me just to make sure I was safe. Two men came and took all the furniture, Trevor paid them and that's why you didn't see him for two days. He told me that you were a kind and understanding family, then he brought me to the shop and you all welcomed me with open arms. How could I not feel and be humble? Your family are perfect."

Trevor said, "I fell in love with her the moment I set eyes on her."

"How could you not, Trev?" David said. "She is a beautiful lady."

June agreed, "All of us are beautiful people – we love life and each other. What is it they say – all for one and one for all? – that is our family. Well, I'm going to eat my scone now and enjoy the beautiful company," said June.

"Oh, by the way, Trev, did David tell you what he had found when I showed him where our den was?" David questioned.

"Yes, a beautiful ring," Trevor responded.

"Ah, I told him to keep it and give it to his girlfriend. Can't imagine how it got there, Trev," David smiled, and winked at Trevor.

Trevor turned his head away to hide his giggle. "I wondered that Dave," replied Trevor.

"What's up with you two?" the girls asked.

"By the way, what did you get up to when you pair went out at night and always came back early morning?" June asked suspiciously.

"Oh, we burgled a couple of houses and hid all of our stolen goods until they were forgotten about; we liked doing that, didn't we Dave?"

"Very funny," June replied. "Ok, don't tell me, I'm not bothered."

"Well, to be honest, we went looking for a couple of nice young ladies but we never found any so we thought we would come back to you and be satisfied with the two lost souls called June and Betty. Didn't we Dave?"

"Yeah, we did."

As June was slapping David across the back of the head saying, "cheeky pair", David pulled her onto his lap, hugged her very tightly, kissed her ear and whispered, "You are the only angel I've ever had or wanted."

June shivered, "Oh Dave, you always make me feel so special."

"That's because you are," he responded.

Trevor pulled Betty close to him. "Yeah, we are the luckiest brothers on God's green earth." Then he kissed Betty on the cheek.

"They are the best, June, aren't they?"

"Definitely," June agreed. "Well we do get on so well together, that's a fact."

Little David came running in from the houses. "I love exploring those old houses," little David ranted.

"David, come here. Do you love them, really love them?" asked his Uncle David.

"I do, Uncle, I love the one you lived in and the one my mom lived in the most."

"Well, my boy, when you are eighteen they will be yours."

"Oh, really, Uncle? Really?"

"Yes," answered his uncle, "but only on the condition that you never let anyone ever change them."

"I wouldn't. If I'm going to own them, Uncle Dave, may I plant the gardens with vegetables?"

"Do you like gardening then?"

"Yes, I've been helping the gardener; he showed me how to do a lot of things."

"I'm really pleased to hear that, David. Did you know that Trevor?" David questioned.

"No, it's a surprise to me as well."

"I will talk to the gardener in the morning and ask him to teach you everything he knows," David decided.

Trevor turned to his brother David and answered, "I know it's not part of our past, Dave, but what do you say to having a potting shed and a greenhouse erected so the gardener can show David how seedlings grow to fully grown plants?"

"That's a good idea; we can put them somewhere in the yard and fence around them so they can't be seen as part of the houses, or we could put them on the end of the garden."

"No," Trevor said, "not on the garden, Dave, that wouldn't be right."

Then June suggested, "That piece of ground across the road, we could buy that, put greenhouses and sheds on it and grow all sorts, then sell them in the store. If David takes to this gardening thing it could be his start to learn about running a business."

"Great idea," Betty agreed.

"Trevor, I will phone the solicitors in the morning and buy that ground and put it in David's name, so then all the profit made can be put into a trust fund until he is eighteen when he will inherit all my shares of the business," David added.

Little David threw his arms around June, "Thank you, I love you so much, I will make you proud of me! Could I borrow some gardening books from the store please?"

His mom told him, "I will buy you any books you want."

"Great," said little David excitedly.

His mom added, "I will ask the gardener tomorrow which are the best books to get for you."

The ground opposite was purchased. When little David saw the greenhouses and the potting sheds being erected he asked his dad if he would employ another gardener. David's dad said, "But we have a gardener."

"He is a veg and flower gardener, I want an expert on tropical plants and trees, I think when I have got the necessary experience I will make lots of profit for the store," little David explained.

"Mmm," said Trevor, rubbing his chin with his right hand. "Yes tropical plants; alright I will look into it for you."

"No, Dad, I've been finding out all about tropical plants, the temperature they need and the easy ones to grow." He started to describe all the plants to his dad and what they needed.

"Oh I see, alright, I will advertise for a specialist gardener in tropical plants."

"May I have a young school leaver as well Dad?"

"You get this nursery erected first, and if I think it's going to work I will see then."

"Oh Dad, please."

"No," his dad answered, "I will get a tropical gardener, now you go and get on with it."

Little David went and started to help erect a greenhouse with the gardener. Trevor went to see his brother David in the wash house. "Hi Dave, I thought you would be in here; it's a wonder you don't move your bed in here."

David laughed, "I know what you mean."

"I've just been talking to little David," Trevor told him. "I think he will go far, he was just trying to get me to employ more staff."

David laughed, "Well he certainly will go far, are you going to get him what he asked for?"

"Yes, of course I will."

"What staff did he ask for?" David enquired.

"A tropical plant gardener, which I think is a good idea, and a school leaver."

"Now that, I like," David agreed. "I think we should let little David try to work that as a separate business, 'David's Tropical Nursery' might be a name for it, what you say Trev?"

"Yeah, sounds alright to me, mind you I will have to ask little David first."

"Listen, Trev," David said, "when you get all the tropical plants and you buy all the fertilisers and compost, make sure there is no peat purchased – we must preserve those peat bogs."

"Too right," Trevor agreed. "Anyway, Dave, why are you sitting in the wash house?"

"I just feel at peace and at home; I was thinking about our mom and Nan."

"Nan?" Trevor said surprised, "She was horrible."

"No, she wasn't really," David reckoned. "We were unruly; she just tried to keep us in check."

"I suppose you're right; we were a couple of rogues, weren't we?" Trevor said.

"Yeah, nobody worse, eh, Trev?"

"Mind you, Dave, we were just trying to survive."

Eight months later little David had his own nursery up and running and making a very big profit. His dad's and Uncle David's store was full of tropical plants. He did name it but it was a different name to what his uncle David suggested. He named it LITTLE DAVID'S NURSERY, because everyone called him little David.

One evening he went to the wash house where his Uncle David was.

"Hello, young David, it's nice to see you."

"Could I have a word with you, Uncle Dave?"

"Yes, of course you can."

"I would like to start up another nursery and I wondered what you would think about it."

"Have you discussed it with your head gardener?" Uncle David asked.

"At length," replied little David.

"Well, what was his conclusion?"

"He wasn't altogether for it, but if you say it's ok I will try to talk my dad round."

"Well, young David, if you believe in yourself and the business I will back you up."

"Oh, thank you, Uncle Dave!"

"But only if your Dad okays it."

Fourteen months later little David opened his second nursery; it went from strength to strength. By the time little David was twenty five he had a chain of nursery's plus the store his dad and Uncle David had given him. Already he was a multi millionaire and just like his Uncle David when he felt troubled, uneasy or even slightly afraid, he would sit in the wash house. In there he felt like his Uncle David was always there watching over him and calming his troubled brow. He sat in his Uncle David's favourite chair and put his feet up, just like Uncle David always did, and feeling calm he drifted off to sleep; all was right with the world. As he started to wake up he felt very calm and relaxed; he just sat and stared until his senses came back to him. He was staring at the roof and thinking to himself that it was good the way the roof all joins together. As his eyes were wandering all around the roof he suddenly spotted a book on a small shelf. Funny, he thought, I don't remember seeing that shelf before. He slowly raised himself up from the chair and reached up to get hold of the book. As he raised his arm and put his hand on the book it slid from the shelf and a cloud of dust covered his face; this made him run outside coughing and spluttering. He blew the surface dust from the book. "Oh, it's a notebook of Uncle David's," he whispered to himself. He knew this, because on the front cover was 'Notes of David's Childhood' Oh yes, I remember now uncle Dave was always writing in a book whenever he was in the wash house and he always closed it up when anyone walked in – he would never say what he was writing about. Going back into the wash house with the book, he sat down in the chair and started to read it. He was so taken to the story he just couldn't put it down – his Uncle Dave had written down everything that he and Trevor got up to, he left no stone unturned as the saying goes. Little David was in more and more shock the further he read into the book. He thought, those sly old devils, and to think I always thought they were dead straight and law abiding. Well, well, he kept saying to himself, and to think I never knew a thing about it. Wait a minute, wait just a cotton picking minute, he was thinking as he very quickly brushed back the pages, I thought so, as he read about the hole in the tip that was his dad's and Uncle David's den. They hid all of their stolen goods in that hole, that's where I found that diamond ring when Uncle David was showing me where the den was that day. Well, my God, and they built our empire from stolen goods! David, by this time, was standing with his hand on his forehead puffing and blowing; he was so shocked he flopped back into the chair, and fell backwards; he rolled over and bounced off the wall. He sat up absolutely bewildered. All he kept saying as he sat on the floor was, "Well I don't know; well I don't know; bless my soul. Suddenly he was aware that someone was standing in the doorway; it was his head gardener.

"Are you alright David?" he enquired.

"Eh? Yes, I'm fine."

"Why are you sitting on the cold floor?"

"Eh? Oh... err, I was... err... I was thinking."

"Those tropical plants from the Congo have all been sold out, will you order them or shall I?"

"Erm, no leave it all to me."

"Alright David, I will clean that middle greenhouse out ready for the new arrivals."

"No," David said, "take the rest of the day off, in fact take the rest of the week off, it's alright, I will pay you, in fact tell the two lads the same, lock up and bring the keys to me."

“Are you sure you are alright David?” asked the gardener.

“I’m fine, honest,” David replied.

That evening as he sat in the house that was his Uncle David’s and his dads, he was gathering his thoughts together. “That’s it,” he suddenly shouted, “that’s what I will do.”

Next morning he called his solicitors and told them to get down to the stores straight away. He got all his staff together; the store wasn’t opened – he told the store manager to put a note on the door saying: ‘Closed Down’. He told all of his staff they were being laid off with a full year’s pay plus an extra thousand pounds each. He got his personal manager to work out all the wages, and by four o’clock that evening each member of staff got a cheque for a year’s wages plus the thousand pounds good will bonus. All the women were crying and the men were in total shock – not one of them knew the reason for the closure, not even the manager. David kept the reason to himself – he was still in shock himself.

That evening all was quiet. David was wrestling with his inner soul. I will go and see the vicar. So off he went, his head full of thoughts. As he approached the vicarage the vicar was just closing the front gate. “Ah, vicar, just the man I want to see,” said David. “How much do you need for your church fund?” David questioned.

“Forty three thousand pounds,” replied the vicar.

“Here is a cheque for two hundred thousand pounds.”

The vicar went white. “Thank you so much!”

“When do you give the down and outs their meals?”

“Every day.”

“Right, how many do you get?”

“Fifty two, same ones every day.”

“Right,” said David, “take them all to a gents outfitters, buy each one a complete new outfit – shoes as well, tell the outfitters to phone me and I will confirm it’s alright and I shall pay them tomorrow evening when they know the amount spent.”

“Are you alright, David?” the vicar asked, concerned.

“Vicar, my way is very light and clear now, my burdens are gone,” David told him.

The vicar had no idea what he was talking about. After he had gone around, helping out all the people he could, he sold all the properties he owned, all except the row of terraced houses and the wash house that his mom and dad grew up in, because he had promised his Uncle David he would always look after them and never sell them. David lived in the house that was his mom's, two doors away from his dad and Uncle David's house.

One evening, many months later, David sat by his fire thinking about nothing special when, and he didn't know why, Uncle David's book came to mind. He got the book from his cupboard and started to read it. I think I will turn this into a novel, he thought.

Next morning he received a letter saying he was to be honoured for services to mankind at Buckingham Palace. David wrote back refusing the honour, for he knew now that what he had given away wasn't really his anyway, it had all been stolen. That evening he started re-writing his Uncle David's memories of fact into a fiction novel. He pondered for ages trying to think of a title, when he suddenly thought, yes, that's it, TWO LITTLE URCHINS.

A poem Trevor wrote for Betty:

When you get married it is for life
When you get married you take on a wife
When you get married it feels so right
When you get married it's really nice
When you get married for ever it is
Through ups and downs
When you have children they are the rose, they are your crown.

Other books by David Prosser:

Pumps With Holes In

Lick 'Em On - I'm Off

Just a Brummie

The Life of David Prosser

Twenty-three Children's Stories